Memoirs of an Undercover Cop
by Frank Santorsola

Miranda Books Inc.
PUBLISHISHED BY MIRANDA BOOKS INC.

ISBN: 9798588149730

This book is dedicated to my brothers in blue.

Thanks to Elizabeth Sidney for editing this book.

Also, by Frank Santorsola

Miranda Writes Honor & Justice

The Garbage Murders

Miranda Writes Honor & Deceit

There's a Gun in my Soup

Miranda Writes/Memoirs of an Undercover Cop

By

Frank Santorsola

Preface

Memoirs of an undercover cop is the title of my fifth book in a series of books. Frank Miranda, is my street name I picked when I was assigned to work deep undercover. I've used the name throughout the series of my books. My first book, Miranda Writes Honor & Justice is about Frank Miranda working with a federal informant who has been convicted of smuggling heroin into New York for one of the five Mafia families in New York City. It chronicles family honor, a tabooed friendship and a surgical look into the very heart of the criminal justice system. The second book is The Garbage Murders, my account of the three organized crime related murders I investigated in New York's private sanitation business. It's my emotional and psychological journey of the choices I had to make to do my job, while simultaneously doing my best to maintain a relationship with the people I loved. Miranda Writes Honor and Deceit the third book that I co-wrote with my wife Christina, tells the story of a terrorist cell intent on killing thousands of people using chemical weapons in New York City. The terrorists learn of Frank's investigation and target him for death. My fourth book, There's a Gun in my Soup chronicles my days in the mob, working as a numbers runner and bookie, where on occasion, I cooked for the wise guys I worked for.

This book, my fifth, is an introspective look into what I'm thinking while I'm entrenched in my deep undercover assignments. It delves into the human condition of what makes Frank Miranda really tick. It was said by a fellow detective that he could never do what I did and truly if my father wasn't such a disciplinarian, I couldn't have. This book reveals why I put my neck on the chopping block and enjoyed doing it.

Chapter One

Every kid dreams of being something when they grow up. I loved watching the Superman TV show as a young boy. I wanted to be just like him. Ultimately, I grew up to become the Chief of Detectives for two District Attorneys in Westchester County, New York that filled the need for me to succeed in my personal and professional life. It may sound corny, but Superman's theme, truth, justice and the American way is what I wanted to bring to my law enforcement career.

They say that we can't escape our formative years and I'm no exception. I have a learning disability and as a result of it had a very difficult time scholastically. I'm dyslexic. It's because of this disability that I struggled with my studies and reading skills in particular. At the time, they didn't have a remedial course in grammar school to address my inability to decipher words in order to help me learn to read.

In the third grade, my teacher, Ms. Rupert, a matronly, broad shouldered woman shamed me when she called on me to read a few pages from an assigned book. I couldn't read a word and she knew it, but called on me anyway, I guess just to embarrass me.

"Okay Frank," Ms. Rupert said. "Pick it up from page ten." I stared at the page for what must have been a minute or so, knowing full well that I could hardly read a word. As the seconds dragged on, I began to sweat and to hyperventilate. Ms. Rupert persisted to press me to read, instead of offering me help for my problem in private.

"Come on Frank," she barked. "Let's begin. You're wasting time." With my head down and sitting silent, I focused on the first sentence. The first two words are still imprinted in my mind. The cat is how the page began. The cat, simple enough for any child to read, who didn't suffer from dyslexia, but it was impossible for me. I tried to sound out the words. I got the word 'the' out, but for the life of me, I couldn't sound out the word cat. Instead, I stammered, "ca, ca, ca"....in a nervous, broken rhythm. All the time that I stuttered, the kids couldn't keep from laughing. Tears streamed down my face as I slammed the book shut. My classmates continued to laugh at me. It was painfully clear that they all thought that I was dumb and sadly to say, I believed that I was stupid too. What Ms. Rupert did next traumatized me for years to come. She walked over, pulled me from my desk chair and dragged me to the front of the classroom. She lifted me onto a wooden stool, propped a pointed dunce cap on my head and had me sit in front of the class for all the kids to laugh at.

In the order of all the demeaning things I would encounter in life, this would rank among the worst. That incident set in motion the fire inside of me that will never be extinguished. Actually, it has pushed me to be successful and to never take no for an answer. Unfortunately, public education at that time, kids like me were pushed from grade to grade regardless of their scholastic ability to advance to the next grade.

Thinking that I was stupid and shunned by most of my classmates, I became belligerent. I developed a reputation of being a tough kid who was constantly in trouble, inside and outside of school. What people didn't know was that I protected myself with an emotional barrier to shield me from most people who thought that I was unintelligent. It was a self-fulling prophecy. I became the kid that my classmates and their parents wanted to avoid. I hated school and despised the daily torment of being viewed as a troublemaker. I'd become an outcast in an educational system that didn't know how to help me. Things were going side-ways for me.

I never opened a book until eleventh grade. I was forced to. My guidance counselor said that I wasn't college material and instead of going to college, I should join the Army. By hook or by crook I was going to college. His criticism reinforced my need to accomplish what I set my mind to and never give up my goal. I was going to show him and everyone else that I was college material. I was going to succeed, never give up and get into a college that would have me. I was going to be a somebody and not let life pass me by. I planned to accomplish things in my life, regardless of the obstacles I faced. I loved taking risks and was ready for my next adventure.

My greatest challenge in life is the written word. I was determined to conquer my dyslexia on my own and somehow teach myself to read. I have accomplished this task and I taught myself to read by memorizing words and their definitions. When graduation rolled around, I was able to stand with my classmates and receive my diploma. With my new victory came new challenges. I finally found a college in Florida that would accept me as a full-time student. I think that the only prerequisite they seemed to have was that you had to have a heartbeat to get in. For the first semester, I was undisciplined and hardly studied. My grades were below a D average and nearly flunked out. I was placed on probation. I decided to put my nose to the grindstone and study. I had to learn a lot of the subject matter that I missed in high school in the second semester. I studied seven hours a day, where most of my classmates only studied two hours. This is where my never give up attitude paid off. I was able to get my grade point average up to a 3.5 and transferred to the University of Bridgeport, in Connecticut.

Something profound happened to me while attending Bridgeport that changed my life. I was taking a course in American History. The course was given in a large lecture hall on campus. I'd taken a written exam regarding the Civil War and was nervous about the results. There must have been some three hundred students sitting in the lecture hall, waiting for the results of the examination. The professor proceeds to call each student up by their last name in alphabetical order. I waited for my name to be called, but when S rolled around, I wasn't called up to pick up my exam booklet. By now, the lecture hall was empty and I was the only one left sitting there. I thought that I must have flunked the test miserably and the professor waited for everyone to leave to tell me how poorly I did.

It was the third grade all over again. Only this time, instead of being dragged up to the front of the class, I was left sitting there like Jimmy the dunce. Finally, I got up and headed for the door. The professor shouted to me, stretching out his hand and holding my exam paper in the air. "Frank, wait a minute, I'd like to see you." Embarrassed, I thought I must have really screwed the test up. I stood there, took the exam booklet, hesitant to open it up. Nothing could have prepared me for the shock of what I saw after opening it. My grade marked on the inside cover was A ++. I was dumbfounded and didn't know what to say. What Professor Charles said next floored me. "Frank, I waited to give you this because it was the best written exam I've seen in years. Your answers to the questions were profound. I wanted to tell you personally that you're a very bright fellow. Please keep up the good work. I'm extremely proud of you."

Professor Charles' comment changed my life completely. He told me that I was bright and at that moment, I believed him. No one had ever told me that before, even though I had taught myself to read, which was an accomplishment. Before that exam, I was a C & D student. After that, my lowest grade in my last two years of college, was B+. Not only had he inspired me, but he softened the hurt from my past, thinking that I wasn't as smart as everyone else.

Chapter Two

There were three families living in my grandfather's house on Fremont Street in Harrison, New York. On the third floor lived my Uncle Louie, Aunt Lena and cousins Gloria and Ronnie. My aunt and uncle were both born in Italy. On the second floor lived my Uncle Domenico, born in Rome, Italy and his wife, my mother's sister, Anita and their son Dennis. My mother and father, brother Rich and I lived in the two-bedroom apartment on the first floor. My grandfather, short and wiry, in his early eighties, was widowed and bounced from one of his daughter's apartment to another, every few months, to keep everyone sane. He was stubborn and used to getting his way with everything. As you'll come to find, he was a free spirit, with a coarse tongue and spoke broken English. When he did speak, his words were fragmented, but he also was fluent in French and German.

I remember the happiness when we lived in my grandfather's house and the happiness it brought, especially during the holidays. We got together and ate Italian meals cooked by my aunts and my mom. They were the three best cooks I ever knew; their cooking would be hard to match in the best gourmet restaurants in New York City. I firmly believe that the way we are raised has everything to do with who we become as adults. My father drummed into our heads precepts like never dishonor your family name, your word is your bond, work hard, respect your elders and stay close to one another. This is the credo I followed though out my life.

My grandfather was a stickler for decorum and brought up his daughters to be refined ladies. He loved opera and during the holidays, sang many operatic songs accompanied by his daughters who sang and played musical instruments. My mom, at the time, was in her sixties, always dressed elegantly and also spoke French, German and Italian. She played the piano. Her younger sister Anita was an angelic soprano, and her older sister Lena played the violin. The four of them entertained the entire family after our traditional Italian desserts of panettone and Italian cake, baked with raisins. There was also cannoli crepes, filled with mascarpone cheese, biscotti and English biscuits. Espresso coffee with a touch of sambuca was on hand to accompany the desserts. Oh, I don't want to forget our traditional game of poker, which was played well into the evening.

My grandfather's homemade wine was a staple in our house that was looked forward to at every meal. My grandfather Guarino was a master wine maker, supervising the process once a year in the basement of his home. The event was a part of my growing up. When I was about 5 years old, enjoying one of the many home cooked meals, my father noticed that we were running out of wine. My father had me go down into the basement and bring up a gallon of red wine.

I left the room and opened the basement door, off of the kitchen. In the basement, I grabbed an empty gallon from the storage area and filled it with wine from an oak keg. On the way up the cellar stairs, the gallon slipped from my hands and smashed onto the steps, sending red wine to the basement floor. I knew that the shit was about to hit the fan. I was in big trouble. Of course, when I re-entered the dining room without the wine and my clothes stained, they all knew I had dropped the wine. My Dad was furious, but everyone else laughed. Standing there, I looked traumatized, like a deer caught in headlights. Thankfully his harangue didn't last long. He turned me around and sent me back to the cellar for another gallon of wine. "Frankie," he said, "this time make sure you hold on to it!"

I have countless stories about my family. Especially the ones involving my grandfather. He was also a risk taker, immigrating to the US from Italy, with no guarantees of supporting himself. I suppose, he's where I got it from. I am a risk taker, somehow, I always seem to find trouble, or it has a way of finding me.

As a kid, about 10 years old, I was still living on Fremont Street and at the time, on summer vacation. My brother Rich was too young and stayed in the house, unless my grandfather, mom, or one of her sisters took him out to play. I remember that it was one of those hot days in August and my cousin Ronnie and I were looking for something to do. On most summer days, my cousin and I would play stick ball in the street, but after a few hours, boredom would set in and we'd look for something else to do. On this particular day, we decided to move into the common driveway and throw the hardball around. No sooner than we began throwing the baseball to each other, the window of the next-door neighbor's house flew open. Mrs. Bonanno an uncouth elderly gray-haired woman, stuck her head out of the window, glared at us with disdain for a second, then yelled, "Frankie, Ronnie, get the fuck out of the driveway, you're gonna break my windows!" Then she slammed the window shut. Being respectful and obedient, we moved out into the street and resumed our catch.

Now, it just so happened that my grandfather was taking his daily constitutional walk, while smoking his favorite Italian cigar, a DeNobili. He heard Mrs. Bonanno curse at us. He stopped for a moment, peered up at her, then slowly continued on his walk.

We weren't in the street for more than five minutes when Mrs. Bonanno open her window again, stuck her head out and yelled, "Frankie, Ronnie get the fuck out of the street before you get hit by a car!" My grandfather heard her, stopped in his tracks and looked back at us. He was clearly annoyed.

Again, being respectful, my cousin and I moved out of the street and onto the sidewalk, in front of Mrs. Bonanno's house. Parked in front of her house was a new Chevrolet Impala that she and her husband Louie had just bought. Not thinking that we might scratch the car by leaning on it, we rested against it as we considered what we were going to do next. Within seconds, her living room window slid open. Ida stuck her head out and screamed, "Frankie, Ronnie, get the fuck off of the car before you scratch it! Go play somewhere else!" She stuck her head back in and slammed the window shut. We were both startled, our bodies reacted by stiffening and we lurched off her car onto the sidewalk. It just so happened that my grandfather happened to be walking by again and couldn't help but to hear Mrs. Bonanno's fowl rant. He stopped dead in his tracks, didn't say a word to me or my cousin, took a long drag on the cigar and proceeded up the walkway to Mrs. Bonanno's front door. He stood in front of her door for a minute and then rang the doorbell. Within seconds, Mrs. Bonanno, dressed in an off-white flowered house coat, nylon stockings and slippers, opened the door. Seeing my grandfather standing there she smiled and said in Italian and English, "Como sti Guraino? What can I do for you?"

In is broken English, my grandfather said, "Ba---Mrs. Bonanno. All-a-day. I hear-a, Frankie, Ronnie, get-a fuck out of the drive-a-way. Frankie, a-Ronnie, get-a the fuck-a out of the street-ta. Frankie, a-Ronnie, get-a fuck-a off-a the car. He paused for a second, looked her square in the face and said, "Ba, Mrs. Bonanno. why-a, you-a go fuck you-self!" She stood there for a minute with her mouth hung wide open. My grandfather, tipped his fedora hat, turned around and walked back onto the sidewalk. We just looked at him as he grinned at us and continued his walk.

Here's another story about my grandfather that I tell fondly. The summer day was hot and humid. I got the idea that a cool glass of my grandfather's wine would do the trick. The cellar was chilly and it was a nice place to cool off and quench your thirst at the same time. I figured that the best way to get into the wine cellar undetected was by way of the basement door, at the back of the house. The only problem was that my grandfather had the door padlocked. My father kept a toolbox in the nearby garage. I removed a hammer from the box, I thought it would do the trick. I was right, a few blows on the padlock with the hammer and bingo, the lock popped sprang open.

We were sitting on folding chairs next to a 55-gallon oak wine barrel, each sipping a glass of cool red wine when suddenly my grandfather lunged through the back door. His face, red with rage and his eyes beaded with anger. He yelled out in his broken English, "Frankie, I-a know it was-a-you idea! Don-a-look-a-my-a-face!" Pointing to his forehead with his index finger, he continued, "You-a-broke-a in! When-a-you father comes-a-home-he-a-gonna-kick your ass-a!" He grabbed me and my cousin by the back of our necks and dragged us out of the wine cellar and into the backyard wagging his forefinger and warning us to stay out of the wine cellar.

There were many incidences like the one I just mentioned, but the one that stands out the most is when we were on our yearly family vacation in Huntington Long Island. My Uncle Louie was the foreman of a New York construction company. The owner of the company had a small cottage in

Huntington Long Island. For one week in the summer the owner of the company would let my uncle use the beach house that sat on 144 acres on the Long Island Sound. The only drawback was that the bungalow didn't have running water or indoor and bathrooms. We got our water from a well that pumps the fresh water that was some 20' deep, situated about six feet from the front door of the house. It was at ground level, with a metal cover and a cast-iron pipe that jetted 4' up from the well. A handle of the pump was attached to this 4" pipe so water could be pumped from the well for drinking and cooking. The outhouse, a small wooden framed shack, sat on top of a deep hole in the ground, another fifty feet from the house. It had all the comforts of home. You may ask, what does this have to do with my roll as an undercover cop? Well, my life experience like the one I'm going to tell you about, shaped me into the person I am.

One late afternoon, my cousin Ronnie and I were bored and decided to slide the metal cover off the well and toss stones into the well as we talked about what we had done earlier in the day. Around 6:00 p.m. my Aunt Lena, Uncle Louie's wife, called us in for dinner. "Ronnie, Frankie, time to eat." She yelled from the front door. We were hungry and of course being just kids, forgot to slide the metal cover back on the well.

Now my grandfather, an early riser, puffing on his DiNobli cigar, stepped through the front door. Dressed in white shirt, necktie and slacks and his trademark Fedora hat that always sat comfortably on his head. I can only imagine the first few minutes of his morning. He opens the front door of the bungalow, breathes in some fresh air coming off of the Long Island Sound, lights his cigar and begins to take his morning constitutional. The sun was not quite up at that time, so surely it was hard for him to see the slate path in front of him. Apparently, he strayed off the path and inadvertently headed in the direction of the well. That's right! My grandfather fell into the well, falling some twenty feet and breaking his leg. He began to yell for help in Italian. "Aiutame, aiutame.!" It means help me, help me. He cried out for at least three hours without being heard, everyone was still asleep. It was about 9:00 in the morning when my mom and aunts were cooking breakfast. I heard my Aunt Lena ask, "Has anyone seen Pop? He's usually up." She asked her daughter, "Gloria, go check Grandpa's room. Tell him breakfast is ready."

Gloria, in her late teens at the time, reentered the kitchen. "Ma, Grandpa's not in his room."

"Maybe he's outside," my aunt replied. "I'll take a look."

I'll never forget what happened next. She stuck her head out of the front door and shouted, "Pop, Pop, time for breakfast." Faintly she heard my grandfather crying out from the bottom of the well. "Aiutame, aiutame." She bolted for the well screaming, "Pop, Pop fell into the well!," as she stared down at him, wet and disheveled.

Eleven of us heard my aunt holler and ran for the front door. Imagine all of us trying to get through a three-foot-wide door at the same time. It was truly a cluster fuck. The adults made it to the well first. Ronnie, Richie, Gloria and I trailed behind. I remember them all circling the well and my grandfather barely able to speak and softly mumbling something in Italian. I pushed my way through the crowd to the top of the well. I looked hesitantly down at my grandfather, flopping around in the water at the bottom of the well. In an instant, our eyes locked. If looks could kill, I'd be dead. Somehow, he found the strength to shout, "Frankie, I-a-know-a it-a was-a-you! You-a-broke-a-my leg-a! You-a-dirty-a- little kid-a!"

My father ran and got a long rope from the near-by garage and tossed it to my grandfather. Everyone is yelling, "Pop, tie the rope around your waist!" He slowly tied the rope around his waist and my father and uncles hoisted him up. As they lifted him, he was completely fixated on me and continually mumbling that I broke his leg. I didn't know what to say but I knew that I was once again in deep trouble. My mom called 911. The local police were dispatching an ambulance.

They arrived in no time. My grandfather was secured onto a gurney and two medics rolled him into the ambulance. From inside the ambulance, he looked out and saw me standing there with the rest of the family and yelled out, "Frankie, no you look-a-my-a-face-a!" The back of the van was finally shut and the ambulance pulled down the long drive out to the main road. Even from that distance I could still hear him shouting that I broke his leg. Like I've said, trouble always seems find me.

I always knew that my folks wanted the best for me and my brother but like so many working-class people, they were too busy making a living. My dad first became a cop but didn't like the hours, so he worked in construction as a bricklayer. My mother helped to support the family by working as a secretary at Arnold Bakers, a bread manufacturer, in Greenwich, Connecticut.

My dad couldn't work during the cold winter months. He collected unemployment checks that financially, just about got us through in those lean months. I remember my birthday was coming up and my dad asked what I wanted for my birthday. On my friend Patsy's birthday, he got a light green Schwinn bicycle with long pom poms hanging from the handlebar grips. I figured, what the hell, I'd give it a shot and ask for a bike. "Pop, I'd like a Schwinn bike like Patsy got for his birthday." Well, he glared at me for a moment, then replied, "What da ya think we're millionaires?" I smirked and then replied, "You asked me Pop."

My dad was authoritarian. Frankly, it took everything he had to keep me and Rich on the straight and narrow. He had an especially hard time with me. I don't know why, but I never liked to be told what to do. In my formative years in school, it seemed that I was in detention on a weekly basis for something or another. That was the way it was for me, even through high school. I was the son who gave my father his gray hair. But in the end, his strict guidance paid off. I was able to work deep undercover assignments.

Chapter Three

I've always liked living on the edge. What I mean by that is that I like taking living in the fast lane. I think it makes life more interesting, at least it does for me. I've always felt that I could think for myself especially in hairy situations, like when I first met Helen. I had graduated Harrison High and was home from college for the summer. I happened to be standing in front of my house talking to my younger brother Rich when Helen rode by on her bike.

"Who's that girl?"

"Oh, that's Helen," Rich replied. "She lives down the street. Helen's in my homeroom class."

"Rich, if she rides by again, I want you to stop her and introduce me."

My brother looked at me and smirked. "Oh, I know you. You want to get to know her."

I looked back, smiled and shook my head in the affirmative. "She's a knockout," I cracked. It wasn't long before Helen peddled towards us. Richie raised his hand for her to stop. We met in the middle of the street and Helen and I talked for at least an hour. Not long after, we began to date. The only problem was that her father was an old school Italian and probably wanted his daughter fitted with a chastity belt. He felt that his daughter was too young to be dating a college man. She was a high school senior and at the time and I was a sophomore in college. I didn't think that our age difference was significant, but obviously her father felt differently. The more her father resisted our relationship, the more I wanted to see her. I asked her out every chance I got. We did the normal things that young people do. We went to the movies, double dated with friends and patronized the local diner, nothing out of the ordinary. We soon became an item by the end of the summer.

The shit hit the fan one Sunday afternoon. As I was leaving my house, about to get into my father's car, her father, at a high rate of speed, screeched to a stop in the middle of the street. The son of a bitch actually jumped from his car and confronted me, nose to nose. Henry, at the time was in his mid-fifties and mean. The ill-tempered creep was short, balding and a face like bulldog. During his tirade, he told me in no uncertain terms that I wouldn't be dating his daughter until she was out of high school or else. "Or else what?" I snapped. "What are you gonna do?" He was a bully and he made no bones about it. If he thought that I wouldn't run the gauntlet, he was mistaken. Sooner or later we were going to butt heads.

"You'll see Frank! You'll see!" He shouted. He got back into his car and sped away. Since I was going back to college anyway, I thought it best to stay away from Helen for a while. Perhaps her father would have a change of heart once his daughter graduated.

That next year, Helen had enrolled in a local business school. I'd come home from college for Thanksgiving break and thought that I'd like to re-connect with her. I decided to give her a call and ask if she'd like to go to a movie on Friday night. I hoped that she didn't have a boyfriend at the time and maybe we could pick up where we had left off.

After Helen and I spoke for a while, I knew there was still that spark of romance between us. By the end of our conversation, I asked if she'd like to take in a movie on Friday night. I was shocked when she said that she'd have to check with her father and let me know. Check with her father, I thought? Something is drastically wrong with this picture. She's no longer in high school and she still had to ask her father if she can go out on a date.

I shoulda known that things were skewed in her family, but I was attracted to her and wanted to date her. When I didn't hear back, I called again. She sounded upset and said that her father told her that she wasn't allowed to date me. I was too old for her. Couldn't date me? That was the wrong thing to hear from a guy who couldn't take no for an answer. There was a pause on the phone for a moment. I still can't believe what I said next. "If your father won't let us date, then lets get married." I have to say I didn't expect her reply. "Okay," she said quietly, "I'll marry you." Well that settled it. We were getting married. It was crazy and all I wanted to do was take the girl to the movies.

On a Monday morning, Helen's parents thought that she was on her way to business school, but in reality, we were running away to get married. Her girlfriend Linda was dropping her off in White Plains to meet up with me. It was about 8:30 a.m. when Helen got into the car I'd borrowed from my father. She looked happy and yet depressed at the same time. I guess she was glad to make a break from her over-possessive father. She threw her schoolbooks in the back seat and we headed for Albany, New York to be married by a Justice of the Peace.

I knew as soon as we walked into our hotel room, I was making a huge mistake, but being me, I couldn't turn back. If I commit to something, I follow though. Plus, remember me, the risk taker. I knew that if Helen didn't return a married woman, I feared that her nutty father would physically hurt her. We were married by the Justice of the Peace three days later. As you'll come to find out later in my story, our marriage didn't survive, but we have two lovely kids from our union. Helen's parents disowned her for a while and we ended up living in a house that I shared with a few college friends while attending the University of Bridgeport. After about six months, Helen was accepted back into her parent's house. As for me, I went along for the ride.

I was able to receive my teaching degree while driving a taxicab during the day and finishing school at night. Soon after my graduation, Helen became pregnant with my first daughter. Preparing to be a father was mind blowing and literally took my breath away. I tried to work as many hours as I could driving the cab in order to save for the baby's arrival. Thank God for my family's support during this time. As I've already said, most Friday nights that I wasn't driving, my brother and I would stop by my Pop's house to chew the fat and have a glass or two of homemade wine while we chatted at the kitchen table. At the time, my brother wasn't married and was finishing up his degree in accounting at Iona College in New Rochelle, NY. He eventually became a Special Investigator for the New York State Organized Crime Task Force.

My father was a blunt man and always quick to the point. He was concerned about Helen being pregnant and that we didn't have health insurance to help pay the doctor and Helen's hospital stay. "Frankie," he said, "you're going to have a baby and you have no medical insurance. You're a college graduate and you're driving a taxicab. I don't get it. You could teach. Teachers have benefits."

My brother just sat there listening as my father continued, "Why don't you take the civil service exam and become a cop? At least you might squeeze by and get health insurance by the time the baby is due."

"I know Pop." I replied. "But, I don't want to teach and I don't want to become a cop. I tried the student teaching thing and I didn't like it. It wouldn't be fair to the kids if I taught and me carrying a gun was out of the question."

Becoming a cop was the furthest from my mind. Most of my friends were rough and tumble guys and some of them had a few scrapes with the law. I wondered how they'd look at me if I became a cop?

"Cop! Pop, I don't want to be a cop!"

"Look Frankie," he shot back. "At least you'll have health insurance and a twenty-year retirement. Believe me, twenty years will go fast and you'll be young enough to do something else with your life."

Not long after our conversation, I reluctantly took the police exam and scored high on the civil service test. I was at the top of list to be hired by one of the police departments in Westchester County, NY. I was called in for an interview by the Commissioner of the White Police Department. One of the requirements in the hiring process was that I meet with the police department's shrink.

So, I soon met with Dr. Karl Bock. Dr. Bock was devoid of any social graces. He was rude, abrupt and small in stature. He wore a forest green corduroy jacket with leather elbow patches, a paisley bow tie and tan slacks. Oddly enough, he focused his questions on my sexual orientation. I think that the bearded weasel was a closet perv who got off on that line of questioning. He asked about my relationship with my mother and females in general. He wanted to know if I had any sexual thoughts of my mother. What did the little troll expect me to say? "Yes doctor, I wanted to screw my mother." I replied, "No doctor, I had no sexual thoughts about sleeping with my mother or anyone else in my family."

He next asked if I had sexual fantasies about my classmates, male or female. Again, what could I say? Straight faced, the dweeb would straighten his bow tie every few minutes, never cracking the slightest smile and go on to the next question. I really thought that this hair-bag was the one who needed a fuckin' therapist, not me. Apparently, I passed that part of my entrance into the police department and subsequently became a cop. However, ever since meeting with that nut job, I'm reluctant to see anyone in the mental health field. Oh, and when my wife gave birth, we had the necessary health insurance.

Chapter Four

Attending the police academy was definitely a learning experience in so many ways. It helped me deal with my life on the street as a public servant. Police officers may be called upon to take a human life in the line of duty. With this in mind, in the academy, I was schooled on the use of deadly physical force. Specifically, article 35, of the New York State Penal Law. It all boils down to using deadly force to protect your life or the life of a civilian. In reality, nothing from a book can prepare you for taking a life. The use of your firearm is surreal. When it's happening, time seems to stand still. Believe me, when a perpetrator is shot, it has a lasting effect on who you are as a person. Thank God our training kicks in, or we may be the ones who are taken to the morgue.

Fast forward for a moment. It was 1:30 a.m. when me and my partner, Willie Serano, a rough and tumble Hispanic kid, in his late twenties were heading home on the Saw Mill Parkway in Yonkers, NY. Willie grew up on the streets of the South Bronx. He was a street fighter who didn't take shit from anyone, especially the city scumbags.

Willie looked over to the median on the parkway and notice two stopped cars with their door wide open. "Frankie," Willie barked, "pull over. I see a person standing in the middle of the parkway."

In the darkness there was a silhouette of a guy standing by two cars that apparently had been in an accident. Willie and I both exited the car and yelled over to the south side of the parkway. "Hey, are you okay?"

The person, whose voice sounded very familiar, yelled back, "Frank, is that you? It's Ron, Ron Sidney." Ron and I were in same class in the police academy.

"Ron, it's me and Willie Serano. What happened?"

"I just got into a fender bender. Four dudes jumped out of their car and ran across the parkway and headed for Dunwoodie golf course. Frank, can you help me locate them?"

"I'll be right over."

For me, this was just another bump in the road. Catching bad guys is what I do. Willie stayed by his vehicle and called the county police for assistance, while I joined Ron on the median. He was standing by his car as I crossed the south side of the parkway and met up with him. Both vehicles had damage, but they were derivable. "Frank," Ron muttered, pointing towards the golf course and said, "they just took off and headed towards the golf course. Help me find them."

We got into Ron's car and took the very next exit off the parkway to the golf course. It was dark and there were only a few streetlights that lit up the road to the main entrance of the clubhouse. Lights were left on in the clubhouse for security. As we exited Ron's car and canvased the area, we noticed the shadows that were hiding in the shrubbery, hugging the side of the club. Ron shouted, "Police, you hiding in the bushes, come out with your hands in the air!" There wasn't any movement for a second or two, then four disheveled men, in their mid-twenties, stood up and walked out from behind the bushes.

One of them, a six-footer, about 200 lbs dressed in what looked like military garb blurted out, "What's up? What'd ya want?" The others stared at us in silence. They were well built and looked like they would have no problem handling themselves.

"I want to see your license and the registration. You left the scene of an accident." I bellowed.

"Fuck you!" The big one shouted. We're not going to show you shit!" After he yelled that, his pals looked at one another for a moment, when the big mouth said angrily, "C'mon, let's get em."

Before we knew it, they were on top of us, punching and kicking and grabbing for our weapons. I smacked the big guy in the head as hard as I could, knocking him backwards, while the other three were on top of Ron. It was a battle royal. The big guy kicked me in the elbow with a karate type kick. I felt my left arm snap. While Ron was able to break loose from the other three, the big guy then turned to Ron, jumped up and kicked Ron square in the face. It sounded like a football being punted. I watched as Ron fell back on his heels. I thought, that's it, it's all over for us. The other three then turned their attention towards me. One of them punching me on the side of my head, while the other two were trying to get to my gun in my waistband. Fuck! I knew that I was fighting for my life. Gripping the butt of my gun for dear life, I actually saw stars and thought I'd lose consciousness. Under the pile of these maniacs, I was able to see Ron, from the corner of my eye, draw his weapon and fire it at the big guy. I actually thought I saw the bullet wiz by, striking the big mouth, who I later found out was Tom Maloney, in the stomach. He looked down at his body for a second, just as a spray of blood shot out of his stomach, like a garden hose had been turned on. Maloney immediately dropped to his knees and fell to the ground. He began to cry for his mother, crying out to her. This only enraged the others even more, as they continued to punch and kick me. Ron was still dazed and reeling back and forth. Just then Willie and the county police showed up. Willie helped them separate everyone. Initially, the county cops didn't know who the good guys were. One of the cops held his pistol to my chest. His nerves got the best of him. His hand was shaking so bad as he rested his finger on the trigger, I thought he was going to shoot me.

Holding my arm in pain, I moaned, "Please put your gun down, I'm a cop. My ID and shield are in my pants pocket." I understand that it was mayhem that night, but the cop was rattled and could have easily killed me. By now, Ron's face was the size of a football. We both needed an ambulance, including Tom Maloney, who would survive his wound. Ron's face was fractured and my arm was broken in two places. I later found out that we were attacked by these mopes because they were AWOL (absent without leave) from the Army. Eventually, my arm healed, but the psychological damage scarred me for life. I'll never take my life for granted and I'll never underestimate how brutal one human being can be to another. Without a doubt, this incident has also taken its toll on Ron. I guess every cop has to deal with these things in their own way. Me, I drank more.

Getting back to my first week in the police department was grueling and I wanted to quit. It seemed that every night I was responding to some kind of death. There was the teenage Asian girl who hung herself in the shower because her boyfriend left her. She was not just a body, but a person with her whole life ahead of her. I won't forget her eyes staring down at me, as she hung from the end a rope tied to the shower head. Then there was the body of a black man, lying in the basement laundromat in the projects, wedged between two washing machines with gunshot wounds to his chest. The sight of him freaked me out. Is this is what being a cop is all about? There were many horrific scenes like this that made me want to quit the force.

Etched in my mind is the elderly man who was hit by a speeding car at 3 in the morning. A young woman who had just left a bar on North Broadway, apparently didn't see him crossing the street and hit him. At the time, I was radioing headquarters and saw the accident happen. She hit him so hard that he flew over her car, sending him some fifty feet in the air. He landed on his back, in the middle of the street. The woman slammed on her brakes, but it was too late. She got out of her car, running back to him and went into hysterics, screaming over him. "I didn't see him! I didn't see him!" The impact was so hard, it knocked him out of his shoes. I called for an ambulance and then ran over to him. He lay there gurgling, trying to breath. Blood poured from his mouth, eyes and ears. I couldn't tell if he was dead or alive and began to give him mouth to mouth resuscitation, waiting for the ambulance to arrive. It was January and about 10 degrees. I wore long johns to keep warm. I can still picture everything so vividly. I'll never forget that night. It's etched in my mind forever.

Lt. James Jenter arrived on the scene and saw that I was an absolute emotional wreck. He immediately relieved me of duty, sending me back to the station house. I was so relieved to be going back to the police station, taking my uniform off and going home. Once in the locker room, I peeled off my uniform. As I started to take off my long johns, I looked down and noticed that my long johns were colored bright red. I was aghast, they were stained from the dead guy's blood. I knew I couldn't take them home and stick them in the washing machine, I couldn't let my wife at the time, see the blood-soaked long johns. I decided to drive to a nearby laundromat and wash them. The blood didn't wash out and I was forced to throw them away. I laid awake all night replaying the dead guy taking his last breath. I never told my wife about the carnage I saw that night, how could I?

The next day the dead man's wife was waiting for me in the station as I was about to turn out. She stopped and asked me if her husband said anything before he died. I lied, I told her that he asked me to tell her that he loved her. I don't know why I told her that, but it felt like the right thing to do.

Another nightmarish incident that I'll never stop thinking about was the traffic accident where a woman's head went through the windshield of her car. She was drunk and hit a tree head on. Her face had been sheered right off when her head went through the windshield. Lt. Jenter, who was in the in the vicinity, responded. When I got there, he was surveying the accident. Sirens were blaring in the distance. Fire trucks were soon driving up to the scene. An ambulance pulled up behind the fire trucks. The woman was still alive and removed from the driver's seat. She was lifted out of the car, placed on a gurney and into the ambulance. Lt. Jenter walked over to me and asked if I had a handkerchief. "Yes Sir." I replied.

"Frank, he said, the woman's face is lying on the hood of the car. Pick it up, put it in your handkerchief and take it to the hospital. Maybe the doctor can sew her face back on."

Looking at what's left of her face, I wanted to puke my guts up. I guess I stopped myself from vomiting because I didn't want to embarrass myself in front of the other cops and firemen. As it turned out, the doctor was able to re-attach the woman's face and I have to say, I felt good that I was able to contribute to her well-being. Soon after that, I think it was the next night, I was assigned to a radio car for the evening. My partner and I got a radio call to respond to shots fired on the second floor of a five-story walk-up. Guns drawn, we slowly walked up to the second-floor landing, noticing that the door of apartment 2J was ajar. Weldon pushed open the door with the barrel of his gun and we slowly entered into the living room. It was dead quiet. There didn't seem to be anyone home. Off of the living room, I noticed that one of the bedroom doors was slightly open. I motioned with my head towards the door. We slowly inched our way to the bedroom. Pushing the door the rest of the way open, we could see a man lying face up on the bed. There was blood everywhere. His intestines lay next to him on the bed. He'd been sliced up from his lower abdominal area to his sternum. He was still alive! Here we go again, more blood and guts. There was no time to wait for an ambulance; a young man in his mid-twenties was dying. We carried him down a flight of stairs to the patrol car. It had been raining that night, so to not get the patrol car soaked with blood, I removed my raincoat and placed it on the back seat. Then laid the poor son of a bitch down on my raincoat. With lights and sirens roaring, we rush him to the White Plains hospital. Unfortunately for him, he was too far gone. We didn't get him there in time to save his life, not for the lack of trying.

I walked into the station house after my tour of duty was over, unbuckled my gun belt and threw it on top of the desk officer's desk. "Lt. Murphy, I quit! I feel like a mortician, not a cop!" I turned and pushed my way through the double doors to the hallway and started to make my way to the stairs that led down to the locker room. Lt. Murphy sprang up from behind the desk and chased me down the hall. He grabbed me by the arm, spinning me around and thrust my gun belt into my chest. I'll never forget what he said. "Frank, I'm speaking to you like a father. I know its been a rough week, but you gotta give this a chance. Don't quit. You're gonna make a fine officer."

It turned out that it was the best advice anyone could have given me. It took a few days for me to unwind from all the psychological trauma and I decided to stick it out. It was the best decision I've ever made. I did give it a chance. In a very short while, I knew that policing was all I wanted to do in life despite all the negative stuff that people had to offer. While working in uniform and dealing daily with underbelly of society, I had become emotionally detached to the death and violence.

As I've mentioned, I loved the Friday nights at my folk's house, shooting the shit with my father. One such night, my brother and I were sitting around his kitchen table, sharing a bottle of my dad's homemade red wine. It was my day off and getting ready for my next swing shift, midnight to eight in the morning. My dad noticed that I wasn't my usual talkative self and asked what was the matter. I was staring into my glass of wine and replied, "Nothing Pop. Nothing's the matter."

"Son, I know you. Something's bothering you."

I slowly lifted my head and told him, "I arrested a friend's brother last night. I'm upset about the whole situation."

"What happened Frankie?", Rich asked. "Well, I was directing traffic on Main Street last night. The overhead traffic light was out and it was raining heavily. I'm wearing white gloves and a bright yellow reflective safety vest. I blew my whistle and raised my hand for the oncoming traffic to stop but this taxicab came barreling toward me. I knew that it wasn't going to stop so I beat feet for the sidewalk. I barely made it. The cabs side view mirror clipped me and I was thrown to the ground. I immediately radioed for a patrol car to stop the cab. It was stopped a few blocks away. When I got to the scene, the driver was already in handcuffs. Winded from running, I was still shaken and pissed. He was obviously drunk and of course he refused a breathalyzer. As he was being placed into the back of the patrol car, he gave me a hard look and said, "I know you, you're Frank. I'm David Vera's brother Chris. You gotta give me a break. If you don't, I'll lose my cab license." I looked him in the eyes and said, "I don't give a shit who your brother is, you nearly killed me! You're drunk! You're going to the can brother!"

My father reached over, took my hand and said, "Frankie, sometimes it's hard to do what's right. You have a job to do. You'll have no regrets in life if you stand up for what's right. Now drink your wine."

Chapter Five

The police commissioner, at the time believed in community policing, so there were many walking posts in the city. Right out of the police academy, I was assigned a walking post in the section eight housing projects. Section 8 housing is for people on government assistance, low-income, disabled and the elderly. My partner and I were responsible to respond to all police calls in the high-rise apartment buildings between South Lexington Avenue and Grove Street. The calls consisted of aided cases like heart attacks and the like. But there were also homicides, stabbings, assaults, robberies, burglaries and drug deals that usually took place in the hallways of the buildings. When the housing projects were first built, the junkies stole all of the copper piping connecting the radiators in the hallways and sold it to buy drugs to support their habit. As a consequence, in the winter, there was no heat in the hallways for the decent people who lived there.

I found out early on that most the folks who lived in the projects respected the cops. We kept them safe from the lowlife's that prayed on them. However, having compassion was a sign of weakness to the degenerate thugs who lived there. My badge number was scribbled on a few of the basement walls, telling these creeps that I was a punk. My partner at the time was Weldon Cheatum, an African-American in his early twenties, who was tall, slender and at the time wore a big Afro hair style. Weldon, had been on the job for five years when we met. He took me aside and told me that I needed to set the record straight with these hoodlums or I'd have a hard time doing my job.

Like I said, we were patrolling the building to keep the law-abiding people safe from the small percentage of criminals who lived in the buildings and preyed upon their own folks. On many a cold winter night, a few of the tenants would invite us into their apartment for a hot meal and warm up. After a short time, Weldon and I built a great relationship with the tenants. They liked and trusted us and they became a great source of information. They knew exactly who did what to whom. There was no doubt about it, I had to establish street creds to earn respect. Soon after Weldon's chat, I picked out the biggest and loudest troublemaker in the projects and arrested him for loitering. He was in the process of shaking down a young black kid for pocket money. The animal was a big bruiser, in his late teens and weighed about 200 pounds. I wasn't sure how this situation was going to play out, but one thing for sure, I knew that he was getting locked up today. Face to face, I asked the punk why he was bothering the kid. The goon was so close to me I could smell his sour breath. He mouthed off and told me to mind my business or I'd get some too. "It's my business slick!" I screamed back. "I saw you shake the kid down for some money. You're loitering and I'm arresting you."

He laughed in my face, shoved me back and told me to go and fuck myself. He began to walk away. I grabbed him by the arm, spun him around and attempted to handcuff him. He thought that he was a tough guy and took a swing at me. I pulled out my blackjack from my pants pocket and hit him square between his eyes. His head blew up to the size of a watermelon. The asshole was handcuffed, charged with disorderly conduct, resisting arrest and sent to the hospital.

The next time I saw him, I was directing traffic on South Lexington Avenue. He looked like the old actor Boris Karloff in the movie, *The Mummy*. His head was bandaged to the point where I could only see his eyes from behind the bandages. The dude made it a point, in front of his friends, to walk over to me and extended his hand. I stared at him for a moment to see where he was coming from, then took his hand and shook it. He said, "Officer, you need information, you come to me." I earned my bones on the street the hard way. I found out that tough guys only respect the use of force.

You gotta learn not to make mistakes on the street. It could cost you your life. After a while you develop a sixth sense about situations that you encounter. You have to, or you're gonna learn the hard way. I was actually able to see shadows of people lurking in the dark. On a midnight tour, I was shaking doors in the business district to make sure that they were locked. As I was going from establishment to establishment, I noticed a car parked up the street with its headlights on. As I approached the car, I saw three males sitting in it. They pointed to me as I walked to the car. They seemed to be agitated. It was unusual for a car to be parked there at this hour of the morning. I walked past the passenger side, out into the street. I made the critical mistake of walking in front of the car. I heard engine roar. As I turned towards the car, it sped forward, hitting me and sending me flying onto the hood and then into the street. I landed hard on my back. The pain was so bad, I thought I actually broke it. Fortunately, my leg took most of the impact. I was dazed and not sure if my leg was broken or not.

A cop on the adjacent foot post saw the incident and called in a 10-13, an officer needing help. The mutts car, an old beat up, rust colored Buick, sped away, but was stopped a few blocks away by a radio car. The three guys in the car put up a fight but were arrested. They were charged with assaulting a police officer with a deadly weapon and driving a stolen car. I was taken to the hospital with a multitude of cuts, scrapes and a leg full of contusions. After being examined and going through a chain of x-rays, CT scans and blood work, I was released in the morning. A court date was set and I testified to the occurrence. The perps, in their late twenties, plead guilty as charged. The driver of the car received the most severe sentence; he was sentenced to three years in state prison. The others had no prior arrests and sentenced to a year in state prison. Like I said, I learned the hard way that night, but I learned.

Chapter Six

After working as a uniformed police officer in the department, I took a job with the Westchester County District Attorney's Office, assigned to their Detective Bureau. I was so excited on my first day of work. A suit and tie were worn by most of the detectives in the squad, unless assigned to the Intelligence Bureau, Narcotics or the Organized Crime Squad. I milled around the squad room for an hour or so meeting other detectives, until me and a few of the other hires were taken to the Westchester County Clerks Office to be sworn in by the county clerk.

Returning to the squad room, the property clerk issued me a 38 caliber Smith & Wesson revolver, holster and a pair of handcuffs. The squad commander said that if I didn't want to carry the issued revolver, I could carry the gun of my choosing. I decided to carry my off-duty gun, a 357 Smith & Wesson 6 shot pistol. At this juncture in my career, I was a seasoned cop. If I had to put somebody down, they were gonna stay down.

At first, I was assigned to a seven-man squad that handled general investigations, ranging from serving subpoenas to trial preparation. After six months in the general assignment squad, Deputy Chief Achim, a mild mannered man, in his mid-fifties with jet black hair, graying at the temples, asked me into his office. He said, "Frank, from now on you're to come in wearing jeans and I want you to grow your hair. You're being transferred to the Intelligence Squad." When long hair was in, my hair was cut short. I guess I've always marched to the beat of a different drummer. I am definitely a nonconformist.

In Intel, I was partnered up with Willlie Serano. We were assigned to surveil known organized crime figures that lived and worked, in and around Westchester County. Willie and I would monitor their daily activities from the time they left their residences in the morning until they were in their beds at night. We'd take notes of who they met with and where they conducted business; trying to put together a criminal case. Our partnership didn't last long though. One day, my squad commander called me into his office and handed me a file, telling me to familiarize myself with Billy

Cohan. He said that the guy runs a pool hall, but in reality, works for the mob handicapping horse races. We want you to try and formulate the criminal activity in the pool hall so that the organized crime squad can launch a criminal investigation.

It was my first undercover assignment and I was thrilled! I wanted to prove my worth and more importantly prove that I could handle the task. As I said, Cohan's specialty is handicapping horse races, nationwide. He works for a Capo in one of the five organized crime families in New York. It's a crime in New York State to give odds and then take bets on the horses racing at the different tracks across the country. For my assignment, I was given an entirely new identity, driver's license, social security number and a vehicle registered in my fictitious name, Frank Miranda.

Billy Cohan was an expert handicapper. He'd analyze the past performances of the jockeys and the horses they rode. Billy calculated the performance of each winning horse and those that placed in each race. Then for the upcoming races, he'd handicap the field of horses, handicap each horse's possibility of winning and pass the information to his mafia connection, who in turn would give the information to his wire room operators taking the horse bets.

During the course of the investigation, one of our informants had first-hand knowledge of two dirty detectives shaking down Billy so he could operate his business without police interference. They'd show up once a week for their $500 payoff. Not only did I have to ingratiate myself with Billy, I had to worry about the cops finding out that a DA's detective was working in the place.

I had learned how important it was to be diligent, not only could the investigation be compromised but more importantly your life could be in jeopardy. This innate talent doesn't come from a book, it's a combination of inherent ability and experience. As always, I loved living on the edge and savored beating these knuckleheads at their own game. It was exciting, addictive and all-consuming.

I began to hang around the pool hall almost on a daily basis, not really knowing what to expect. The pool hall was on the second floor of a five-story building on Third Avenue in Mt. Vernon, NY. I introduced myself to some of the regulars and began to shoot pool with them. I was extremely conscious of how they reacted to me and tried to get a feel if they bought my persona. Luckily for me, I knew how to shoot pool. Growing up, I used to play with friends all the time. The guys seemed to like me and thought that I was one of them, a knock around guy that didn't have a steady job. Of course, they wanted to know who I was, what I did for a living and where I came from. Some of them were junkies who sold drugs to survive and support their habit. I said that I'm living in the north Bronx and drove a truck, delivering furniture for a furniture manufacture in New Rochelle, but business was slow. Right now, I'm collecting unemployment checks to tide me over.

I had been shooting pool for about a week, when Billy stopped me as I walked in. He asked if I wanted to enter a tournament that he was promoting. "Frank, the guys that you play with have entered. Why don't you?"

I shot pool pretty well and replied, "Sure Billy, why not?"

"The entrance fee is $25.00," Billy said. "If you win, you'll get half of all the entry fees. I keep the rest."

Billy walked back behind his desk and grabbed a few sign-up sheets and handed them to me. There was a line for your name, address and phone number. Now that I think of it, it must have been a ploy to get my personal information to see who I was. Just as I was about to fill it out, the phone behind the desk rang. Billy turned his back to answer to wall phone. As he spoke, I began filling out the sheet. On the very first line where my name went, I jotted down my real name, instead of my fictitious name. I almost shit my pants when I realized what I had just done. I started to panic, but was able to regain my composure. I quickly crinkled the sheet up into a ball and put it in my pocket. Billy must have heard the crumpling of paper and turned around. He hastily remarked, "Frank, what happened to the sheet that

you were filling out?" I was quick to respond. I replied, "Oh, I put my old address down, sorry." I took another sheet from the stack on the desk. I then reached in for my wallet and peeled off $25.00, handing it to him.
Fuck me! What a learning experience. I could have blown everything. This experience reinforced the fact that I had to focus on my mission all the time. I had to develop, as they say, the eye of the tiger. I learned that if you let your guard down just for a moment, you're done. I've got to become the person that I'm pretending to be. Literally, that day I became Frank Miranda, a street guy who lives by his wits.

On the day of the tournament, I was competing against the skells that I shot pool with. I wasn't ten minutes into the first game when I noticed two men, one white, one black, wearing fedora hats and gray overcoats standing by the front desk. They were speaking to Billy. I noticed that Billy flicked his head towards me. They looked over and gave me a suspicious glance. Several minutes passed and then the two guys walked over. The black guy yanked out a police shield from his jacket pocket, shoved it in my face and said, "We're detectives from the Mt. Vernon police department." The other one asked to see some identification. I pulled out my driver's license from my wallet and handed it to him.

I asked, "What the hell is this all about?"

He barked, "Oh, you're a smart ass! Keep your mouth shut! I'll let you know when you can talk."

"I ain't no smart ass! Why you hassling me?"

He got so mad, I thought he was going to spit. He grabbed my arms and literally picked me up and threw me on top of the pool table, pushing my face into the felt. As I lie face down, the black detective went through my pockets, tossing everything onto the pool table. My instincts told me that they were looking for a police shield. Of course, they didn't find one. All they found was my phony identification. Both detectives took turns thumbing through my ID and intensely scrutinizing it. Then, they grabbed me and dragged me off of the pool table and into the men's room, where they literally ripped my clothes off. I'm sure that the scumbags were looking to see if I was wearing a wire. Believe me, I was pissed off. "What the fuck, man? I screamed! "Why are you doing this?" These assholes are supposed to be cops, but in reality they're worse than the scumbags that were paying them.

"Keep your mouth shut!" The white detective bellowed as he twisted my arm behind my back.

"What the fuck did I do?" I shouted.

The black detective shot back "You're a new face in town and we want to know who you are." He bent over and picked up my blue jeans, tossed them at me and barked, "Don't be such a wise guy!" They walked out of the bathroom as I was getting dressed.

I was loaded for bear as I walked out of the bathroom. My gut told me that these pricks weren't done with me yet. Billy didn't say a word as I walked past him towards the door. It was obvious that there was no love lost between us. He gave me a hard stare as I walked out of the door and it closed behind me. The informants tip about corrupt cops in the joint was on the money. I knew that these two birds would be waiting for me as soon as I walked out into the street.

I'd found a parking space earlier, right in front of the pool hall. It seemed that my head was on a swivel, looking for these two assholes. It's not every day that you're tossed by cops. I was so mad, I could taste my bile. As I stared at the car and slowly pulled out into traffic, I looked into the side view mirrors to see if anyone was tailing me. Sure enough, these two cocksuckers pulled out right behind me in a Ford Galaxy.

I planned to give these corrupt sons of bitches a run for their money before ditching them. I stopped in a deli on Third Street and ordered a sandwich.

After I left the delicatessen, I parked in front of an OTB (Off Track Betting) parlor on White Plains Road in the Bronx and placed a few horse bets. Every time I pulled over and parked, they'd followed suit. Finally, I had enough of their shit and decided it was time to lose them. I circled the block a few times until I lost them in the heavy traffic. When I was sure that I lost them, I took the back streets to my office and reported the incident to my squad commander. All Captain Matthew said was, "Good job Frank. We're gonna get these guys."

"Damn right Cap!" I replied. "They don't deserve to wear the badge!"

It took all the moxie I had to return to the pool hall. I had to maintain my cover and not blow the investigation. Billy kept me at arm's length, it was obvious that he didn't trust me. Every time the door opened, my heart stopped, wondering if it was the two assholes returning to hassle me.

In the end, as a result of my work, my office had probable cause to place a wiretap on Billy's business phone. The case ultimately was presented to a grand jury. Unfortunately, and I don't know why, no indictments were handed up, so no one was prosecuted. However, there was no doubt in my mind that Billy Cohan was running an illegal gambling operation for the mob and the two detectives that harassed me were on the take.

Chapter Seven

Working in the District Attorney's Office's detective squad is a lot more complicated than working in uniform. There were many more personalities to deal with in the DA's office than in the police department. For example, in each investigative squad there's an Assistant DA assigned and they oversee each case to its completion. At times, legal issues may surface during an investigation that leads to a conflict in strategy between the detective working the case and the ADA. This dispute now brings into play the squad commander and sometimes the Chief of Detectives. It can be like walking on eggshells for the detective who's now in the middle of the mix and the layers of people who may have a different perspective on how to solve the matter at hand.

Things in the DA's detective squad can go sideways in a moment's notice. The one case that comes to mind is when I was in the middle of a multi-kilo cocaine deal at the Cross County Shopping Center in Yonkers and the Colombian coke dealer decided that he didn't like the location. Out of the blue, he picked another location about a mile away. This in and of itself was a dangerous move for me, but again a learning experience. My backup was geared up for the buy to go down at the Cross County Shopping Center and unaware of the change of the location. I had to communicate the new location. It was in the rear of the Key Foods Supermarket on Yonkers Avenue.

I didn't blink an eye about the change in plans, but deep down inside my guts were churning. I didn't know if my back up team heard my transmission. If they didn't, then I was on my own, which wasn't a good place to be. It was just me and the 357 magnum I had hidden under the front seat of the Firebird.

On the ride over to the supermarket, I had to keep my nerves in check. I had to stay cool to make this thing work. If I survive tonight, I plan to belly up at some bar and drink a bottle of Jameson Irish whiskey to relieve the pressure I'm under. We all know to self-medicate isn't a good thing to do, both mentally and physically, but it seems to have worked for me at the time.

As soon as I had a chance, I transmitted the change of location and headed for the supermarket, hoping that the enforcement team was right behind me. I couldn't have been more wrong. They never got my transmission. By the time I got to the supermarket, the Colombians were anxious to see the money. All the while, I'm thinking that the enforcement team is secreted somewhere nearby, listing to our conversation, waiting for my signal to lock the assholes up. I tested the coke and signaled for the arrests, but nothing happened. The head guy got hyper anxious and wanted to see the money in the trunk of my car that contained $28,000. The other two shit birds remained in the Mercedes S 550, while I tried to stall El Jefe, a ruddy face, pot marked man, in his mid- twenties.

"C'mon Popi, the money!" He screamed.

"Okay, okay," I yelled and threw up my hands in the air, as if to say, wait here a second. At that moment, I knew I was on my own. The backup team wasn't coming and I knew what I had to do. With my hand still in his face, I walked back to the drivers side door of my car, opened it, reached under the front seat and grabbed my 357 pistol. I then hustled back to El Jefe and stuck it in his face. I wish I could describe the look of panic he had. I grabbed him by his sweatshirt, turned him around and forced him back to his car. I shouted for the other two monkeys to get out of the fucking car. "Don't move a God damn inch, you're under arrest!" Reluctantly, they slowly got out of the car, their faces ashen gray as they dropped their handguns at their feet. I don't know why they didn't shoot me. I really thought that this was the end of the line for me. God must have been with me that day. Finally, the backup team arrived, managed to apprehend them and brought them back to the office for processing.

On the drive back to the office I got sick to my stomach and pulled over to the shoulder of the parkway and threw my guts up. Deep down inside, I wish I had someone in my life that I could talk to. I wish I could open up and tell them that I was afraid for my life today. I'd tell them that I was involved in a buy/bust operation that didn't go as planned. I'd tell them that I might have been killed today. I want to let go to someone and explain how I feel inside. How shit like this eats at me and keeps me awake at night. How sometimes I wake up in a cold sweat and afraid to go back to sleep for fear of more nightmares. How the only relief I get is in a bottle of scotch.

Oh some might say, talk to the office shrink or a family member. But I went that route, talking with a shrink when I joined the police department. Believe me, I don't think the guy could help himself, let alone help me. As for family, they'd tell me to quit and to find something else to do with my life. I've considered all my options and came to the conclusion that this is who I am and what I want to do for the rest of my life, regardless of the upheaval it causes.

I guess I've gotten a little ahead of myself in this story. As you already know Frank Miranda is my fictitious name. I'll tell you how the name came to be. One day, when I was bullshitting with some of the guys in the squad room and the Chief of Detectives at the time, Shawn Daniels, walked into the squad room and asked me to follow him into Intelligence squad. On the rear wall of the room was a rogues gallery of the five organized crime families in New York. Shawn, a hulk of a man, in his early sixties, 6 foot five, 260 pounds with balloon bags hanging under his eyes from the stress of his job, walked up to gallery of photos. Each family was framed in a large chart with the mugshot of each family member. That's the day Frank Miranda was born.

"Frank," the chief said, pointing to the charts. "Pick out a name from one of the families, any name. That's your name from now on."

I didn't realize the implications of what the chief was saying or what was involved in assuming a new identity and the work that I was about to undertake. I perused the charts and settled on the name Frank Miranda, a soldier in the Genovese Crime family. I liked the sound of the name, it felt comfortable.

As fate would have it, I later found myself working deep undercover, infiltrating one of the crews one of the five families. It was a piece of cake. These guys are all about money. I have half a brain and I knew I could make them money, they're all about money. Most importantly, I grew up in an Italian American household. As a kid, I was taught to listen. With these guys, I knew when to talk and when to keep my mouth shut and I was streetwise. I grew up hanging around with my friends on the streets and knew my way around. One thing for sure, you gotta be real because you can't fool these guys. They know a fugazi, or in laymen terms, a fake when they saw one. They aren't stupid, on the contrary, they are extremely smart. As I've already said, you gotta be real, your life depends on it. After a while I stopped looking at these guys as people, just targets.

Chapter Eight

It took some time, but I eventually started to feel comfortable in my role as Frank Miranda. My transition from the police department to the District Attorney's office was relatively a smooth one, but as I came to find out, working deep undercover comes with a price. The stress from the work, combined with trying to maintain a normal family life is hard to do. There are the late hours, hanging out in bars and strip clubs, where it's easy to get involved with other women, definitely problematic for any relationship. As it turned out, most of the guys in the squad were divorced or on their way to becoming divorced. It came with the territory. My children suffered the most when my marriage to Helen broke up. We're estranged even today.

I'll never forget ringing my mom's doorbell early one morning when Helen asked me to leave the house. She answered the door dressed in her usual housecoat. When she opened the door, she looked down at my suitcase and immediately knew what was going on. We stared at each other for a minute or so before she asked, "Where's Helen and the kids?" I knew that my mom was just rubbing it in by her question.

"Ma, Helen kicked me out."

I'll never forget what she said to me next, "Frankie, I have two sons; one is the good one and one is the bad one. Guess which one you are?"

"Ma, I need a place to stay for a few days. Can I come in?"

Finally, in Italian she replied, "Vieni a casa, Frankie."

Walking into my old bedroom I thought, I'm right back where I fuckin' started. My divorce from Helen was rough. During the divorce proceedings, I sat on one side of the courtroom with my lawyer and Helen sat on the other side with hers. Helen's lawyer stood behind an old oak table and read a list of the household items that Helen wanted after the sale of the house. Her pencil neck lawyer read, "My client will keep the kitchen set, the dining room set, the living couch and chairs." I looked over at my lawyer, waiting for him to object, but the knucklehead sat mute. I nudged him with my elbow a few times, but he didn't react. Frustrated, I jumped up, raising my voice and said, "Your honor, what about me? What do I get?" He glared at me for a second or two and said, "Mr. Santorsola, if you don't sit down and be quiet, you'll get jail. Do you understand?" I sat back down, dejected and ultimately signed the divorce decree, walking away with absolutely nothing. That was just the beginning of all the drama between me and my ex-wife. She took me to family court so many times to reduce my visitation rights that eventually the judge got sick of her antics and awarded me more visitation time to spend with my girls.

It was extremely hard for me to be forced by a piece of paper not to live with my kids. After all, I wasn't divorcing my kids. In retrospect, leaving my kids was the hardest thing I ever had to do in my life. Believe me, infiltrating the Mafia was less stressful. People asked if I was ever afraid while working with these guys. My reply was, they can kill me, but they can't eat me. They wanted to know what that phrase meant. My answer was, "It means that you can't eat from an empty plate. The court took everyone I love away from me. I have nothing left to lose."

Chapter Nine

I've been working undercover narcotics for a while when I was summoned to the fifth floor of the courthouse. The District Attorney called an impromptu meeting. Chief of Detectives Daniels was already seated when I was buzzed into her office past the DA's assistant, Jennifer, a smartly dressed, long legged brunette in her mid-thirties.

The DA, an attractive woman in her late forties, with her hair tied in a bun and sparkling brown eyes was seated behind a large mahogany desk that centered her office. The chief motioned with his hand and politely asked me to pull up a chair. We made small talk for a while, then DA Larson came straight to the point. "Frank, there's a Lucchese crew that holds court in a social club on Willow Street in South Yonkers. We think that you're the right guy to infiltrate the crew."

I'm thinking like what I'm doing isn't dangerous enough. Now they want me to get into bed with wise guys who'd kill a cop without blinking an eye. I'm certain that Larson needs an organized crime case in her coffers for her re-election campaign next year. I'm just a means to her end.

The Chief followed with, "Frank, we've been monitoring your work and feel that you're the right fit for this assignment as DA Larson said. We'll give you all the tools you'll need to make this work. What do you say?"

I have to admit, I was concerned about the assignment. More importantly, I was concerned about the consequences. Like I said, these guys don't play games and have a long memory. Fooling drug dealers for a few days is one thing, but living a double life with the mafia is a whole other ballgame. I'd have no schedules and no regular reporting system, which in all honestly, I liked. I'd be responsible to myself, living by my wits with no backup, an island unto myself.

"Can I think about it?"

The chief, his impatient self, answered, "Sleep on it overnight and give me your answer in the morning." The prick knew what my answer would be. I had to take the assignment, or he'd find a way to make my life miserable. Not only did I have to contend with a divorce, but now I was embarking on another life.

That night I didn't get much sleep. I wondered if I could actually pull it off. I had a pretty good idea what these guys are about. They lived and worked in the neighborhood I grew up in. Power, money and violence is their social statement. After tossing and turning for eight hours, it was time to face the day. The upside of the assignment was to prove to the world that not all Italian Americans are members of or associated with the mob. Last year when checking into a hotel in Albuquerque New Mexico, a hotel clerk said without reservation, "Oh, your last name is Santorsola, you're Italian, are you associated with the mafia?"

I mentioned earlier that I was given a phony identity when I was sent into the Billy Cohan's pool hall. Frank Miranda is who I am, a knock around street guy up from Florida. I began to hang around the Yonkers neighborhood, renting an apartment on Oak Street, a few blocks from the social club. I didn't sleep for months while I attempted to ingratiate myself into Calise's crew. Falling asleep every night in the shit-hole of a rented apartment was a task. I'd replay every word that I uttered to these lowlife's during the day. I worried constantly that they would pick up on something I've said that might give me away. One thing's for sure; they hated cops and informers. If they found out that I was a cop, it could have cost me my life.

Mickey Calise and his crew of criminals were smart and could smell cop a mile away. I was the new guy on the block, and they wanted to know everything about me; where I was living, where I came from and how I make ends meet. Before I was accepted into the life, I was tested on a daily basis for a year. They'd bump into me and rub up against me, trying to see if I was carrying a gun or wearing a wire. My phone records were checked, and they contacted their guy in the Department of Motor Vehicles to see if the car I was driving was registered to me. They even had some dirty cop break into my apartment and look for anything that said cop. I'll never forget the day that Mickey handed me a large amount of money in the social club. We were sitting at the bar, eye to eye and he slid a stack of large bills in front of me. Mickey said in his sinister voice, "Frank, we know you're a cop, take the money and get the fuck out of here." I kept it together, grabbed for the money and said, "I'm not a cop, but I'm gonna take your money anyway." I had the money in my hand and started for the door when he jumped up and snatched it out of my hand.

"Look Frank," he said, "I gotta make sure that you're not a cop. Our thing depends on it. Capisci?"

"I know Mickey. I got no use for them either."

I knew then that I could handle anything that these guys through at me. Living on the edge is one thing but the daily roller coaster ride of emotions really took its toll as time went on. I tried to sleep, but I couldn't. I tossed and turned all night. I'd lay in bed and wait for daylight to roll around so I could get to the club and see how I'd be received. No matter what they threw at me, I knew that I would never give up, I was all in. I was going to see this thing through to the end no matter what.

One night I was sitting in the neighborhood bar and grill having a beer. This thug walked in and got into an argument with the bartender, pulling a knife on him. It was late and I was the only one at the bar. The bartender knew that I lived in the neighborhood and sometimes hung out at Mickey's club. I decided to step in. I figured that this was a good way to establish my street credibility. I didn't know how this thing was going to shake out. I stood up, telling the jerk to put the knife away and relax. He sat a few bar stools away. Now, directing his attention to me, he slowly walked over and pushed the shiv into my ribs, barking, "You want some, slick?" Fuck, I was trembling inside, but I couldn't let on. I looked the guy square in the eye and said, "Look friend, you stick me, you're going to jail. Why don't you put the knife away and let me buy you a drink? We'll walk out of here friends."

I found out later that John White had just been released from state prison. He did ten years for manslaughter; killing a guy with a knife in a bar fight. John smirked, then put the knife away. I bought him a few beers and later that night we walked out of the bar together. Just so you know, my insides still tangled in knots when I think about it. There was a good possibility that I wouldn't have walked out of the bar that night. Word of the incident spread like wildfire. The very next day Mickey sent for me. Mickey held court in the back room of the social club. When I walked in, one of the guys said, "Frankie, Mickey's in the back."

Mickey was sitting at a small circular Formica top table that was illuminated by a 50-watt light bulb suspended from a frayed electric cord. He motioned with his head to pull up a chair. "Frank, I heard what you did last night in Bobby's bar, thanks. Bobby is a friend of mine and because you stood up and showed me what a man you are, I want to give you an opportunity to make some good money. I'd like you to take over a numbers spot in the Bronx and I'll even give you money to lend on the street."

Bingo! I was working for Mickey. It was an emotional high. It's hard to explain, but I got a rush just knowing that I was now one of them, one hurdle at a time. I knew that my office would be licking their chops that I was in Mickey's crew. I'd be the instrument that DA Larson needed for probable cause, which afforded us the ability to use bugs and wiretaps. I was privy to Calise's social club. He ran a poker and craps game every day. Mickey took 5% of every bet made on each hand of poker played or every roll of the dice. In New York State, it's illegal to cut the game.

Freddy Spina and me became close. He had sixty plus years of wise guy experience. Spina could have played one of the characters in the movie, *The Godfather*. He dressed casually in slacks, a sports shirt and wore a fedora hat. Freddy also worked in the numbers game and also was a loan shark. You could find him hanging around card and craps games, lending money at usurious rates of interest to degenerate gamblers. He was always looking for new customers and I made sure that I fit the bill. I hate to say it, but I liked Freddy. His sense of humor relieved much of the daily stress I faced.

It's amazing how things can change on a dime in my line of work. An excellent example was when I started making money for Mickey, it blinded him. I became one of his favorites. He even invited me to his house to meet his wife, his son and his daughter. I was there for many home cooked meals on Sundays. He treated me like one of the family. Believe me, it twisted me inside knowing that in the end he would be arrested. On occasion, I was asked to wear a wire. The only caveat was if it was found I was in trouble and there was no help around. I wore a state-of-the-art wire one day. It was the latest technology, called The Ghost. It's used in conjunction with an iPhone app and a tiny device strategically worn on the inside of my belt. The end result was nothing short of a spectacular audio and video. I double checked my phone in the club's bathroom to make sure that the devices were in sync. Under pressure, your mind can really play tricks on you. Is my phone on? Is it at the right setting? Then there's what happens to me if these psychopaths find it? I'd probably end up in some landfill somewhere.

On that day, there were five or six of us shooting dice, hovering over the craps table. Freddy had the dice in his hand about to roll them, when the front door flew open and a uniformed Sgt. walked in. He stood there for a moment with a grin on his face. The Sgt. was a big man in his own right, 6' 3", 200 lbs. He wore a black leather jacket, puttees, and black boots that a motorcycle cop would wear. I thought, along with everyone else, that the game was about to be busted. What happened next shocked the hell out of all of us.

The Sgt. walks up to Mickey and says, "Mickey, from now on I get 10% of the game or you don't run the game. That goes for your poker and Ziginette games too. I'll stop by every Friday to collect. I gotta pretty good idea what your take is." He stretched out his arm cross the craps table, scooped up about $2,000, put the money in his pocket and walked out the door. What he didn't know was that I was in the joint and wearing a wire. Mickey went wild. He ranted and raved about the Sgt. for an hour. He squawked, "The fuckin' cops are worse than us."

At the end of the investigation, the Sgt. was arrested and indicted for extortion and Grand Larceny. He ended up losing his job and his pension.

He wasn't the only cop caught up in the web of corruption during my time in the mob. There were a few more. Now, I don't only have to worry about the mob guys, I gotta worry about the cops that have lost their jobs because of me. I've learned that people are people and money makes them do things that they may not have ordinarily done.

Chapter Ten

Mickey set me up in a numbers hole in the back room of a fruit and vegetable store on 3rd Avenue and 153rd Street in the Bronx. I took bets over the phone and from people in the neighborhood who patronized the fruit store. To explain the numbers game, it's an illegal lottery run by the mob, with profits invested into the purchase of narcotics, loan sharking, political corruption and the infiltration of legitimate businesses to launder their dirty money.

After a few months, I was knocking down a lot of money from my numbers business. After my customers were paid, Mickey received 70% of the net money and I got to keep 30%. My end went directly into the DA's coffers; I never kept a nickel. Mickey loved me. I was a big earner and I enjoyed the respect I got from Mickey. When you're an earner, you can do no wrong, even bending one of their rules, which are simple, protect their society, never cooperate with the police, always be at their beckon call and never make advances towards their wives and daughters.

Everyday folks can bet daily on their favorite number to win. The winning illegal number is calculated from either of the two New York racetracks. The New York number, as it's referred to, is derived from Roosevelt Raceway in Westbury, Long Island and the Brooklyn number is calculated from Aqueduct Racetrack in Jamaica Queens. Some betters prefer to bet on the Brooklyn number and some like to bet on the New York number. The winning numbers are posted everyday by the numbers bank that computes the winning numbers.

Most of my customers were Hispanic. I'd gotten to know them and their families personally. They liked me and I liked them. We had a mutual respect for one another. Most of them were hard working people who tried to get ahead financially by betting on their favorite number. Some of them bet the month and day of their birth and some bet on a number they'd dreamed about. If they won, I'd pay them the very next day. The payout was

600 to 1 on a straight bet and 30-1 on a combination of numbers. A $1.00 straight for example on the number 357 would yield a payout of $600.

If the bettor decided to bet 357 in combination and 735 came out, it would pay $30 into his/her pocket. Me personally, I loved the everyday action. I began to live for the high that working deep undercover gave me. I'm the type that can never sit still, so dealing with my customers and the wise guys every day kept me on my toes and my adrenaline flowing. My business grew tenfold in a short time. During that time, I was only responsible for myself and that felt good. I respected the code of honor they lived by. There was no deadwood in mob life, either you earned for them or you were out. If they felt that you had betrayed them, you were killed and found ten toes up on the sidewalk or in the trunk of your car.

It's a misconception that everyone in the mob is a killer. For example, most of the guys that I knew in the numbers racket were just knock around guys who didn't want to make an honest living. They took the easy way out or so they thought and they weren't violent people. I have the ability to look at a person and know if he or she is dangerous or not. This quality guided me through many dangerous situations I faced. But like anything else, it's a work in progress.

I gained some insight into how these mopes operate. I've mentioned that a uniformed Sgt. had been shaking down Mickey for protection. On Sunday nights, Mickey held an Italian card game at his club, called Ziginette. Every gangster in the New York metropolitan area attended this high stakes game. Thousands of dollars were bet on each hand played. The game is played similar to Punto Banco or Baccarat with three decks of cards dispensed from a wooden shoe. $500 gets you a seat at the table. The house never loses, it gets 5% of every hand drawn. The fact that the house took the 5% cut made the game illegal in the State of New York.

What happened to me one Sunday night still vibrates in my brain. I was watching the game from behind one of the seated players, when this wise guy, Foxy, had a $10,000 bet on the next card drawn from the shoe. I think he needed a king of hearts to double his money. If the king wasn't the next card pulled, he'd lose ten grand. The next card wasn't the king of hearts. Foxy lost his $10,000 to the house. I made the huge mistake and commented on his loss in all sincerity, "Oh, that's too bad Foxy." It just blurted out of my mouth. Foxy looked at me with the look of death in his eyes. He jumped up from the table and yelled, "Too bad, too bad!" and pulled a 25 caliber automatic pistol from his waist and pointed it square at my forehead. I swear he was about to pull the trigger when Big Paulie, who sat next to him, jumped up and grabbed his arm, pushing his gun hand to the floor. "Foxy, give the guy a pass, he works for us. He didn't mean anything by it." If looks could kill, I'd be lying on the floor with a bullet in my head. Foxy, his face beat red, his face contorted with rage, sat back down. I wondered if the guys in the club could hear my heart pounding. I thought my heart would blow through my chest. If he shot and killed me that night, no one and I mean no one would know what happened to me. Not my office or my family. All they'd know is that I had disappeared. It might take years to find out what really happened to me. Maybe they'd discover that I was murdered from a cooperating witness, who got jammed up with the law and was looking for a way out of his trouble. In any event, I'd be dead and there's no coming back from the grave. They say that your life flashes in front of you when you're about to die. Well, mine didn't. The only thing that flashed in front of me was getting out of the club in one piece and knocking down a few tumblers of scotch.

Chapter Eleven

Mickey, at the time was in his late fifties, short in stature, weighed 250 pounds or so and worked out regularly. He loved expensive clothes and had a sophisticated look about him, but in reality, he was a classic psychopath. The social club offered Mickey and his associates a secure place to meet. It's on the first floor of a two-story red brick building, in an urban neighborhood, with a lot of foot traffic on the street. The club phone was wiretapped and bugs were placed in the light fixtures and electrical sockets throughout the place. My office had been recording the conversations for months. Ever since the incident with Foxy, I had cold sweats every time I walked into the club, especially when I wore a wire.

I'd been working for Mickey for about two years and I have to say, he treated me like a son. He even introduced me to his daughter Maria. Maria, in her early thirties, was five by five; five feet tall and five feet wide and was looking for a husband. She had a black mole on her face the size of an Oreo cookie. It took a lot of bobbing and weaving on my part not to get involved with her. She and I spent a lot of time together, socializing at weddings, wakes and at her father's house for Sunday dinners. She's made her feelings known many times; I had to tread lightly. If I came right out with it and told her that I wasn't interested and it got back to her father, I could find myself in deep shit. One day, Mickey took me aside and said that if I married Maria, I could punch my ticket in this thing of ours. I had to fess up and tell him that with all due respect, I don't think I'm the marring kind, but maybe in a year or so, I'll rethink it. This would buy me some time as the investigation was winding up. Mickey gave me one of his bone chilling stares and said, "Yeah Cheech, you think about it. My daughter's lonely and needs a husband."

It seemed like everyday something would go wrong. I was wired one day with a transmitter, powered by a nine-volt battery that was taped to my chest. As soon as I walked into the club, it began to leak battery acid. The acid slowly burned a hole in my chest, around my solar plexus. I was on fire, but I had to conceal the pain so the guys wouldn't notice that I wasn't my regular self. I began to sweat profusely. I had to constrain myself to keep my body from shaking. With beads of sweat pouring down my face, one of the guys asked if I was okay. "Cheech, he remarked, it's cold in here. Why are you sweating?"

"I think I'm coming down with the flu." I gave a fake cough.

Fortunately for me, he and everyone else bought my story. I stayed in the club for another 30 minutes before I could leave. I ripped the transmitter off as soon as I was out of sight and hurried to a designated location where I met up with the detectives who were supposed to be recording the conversation. In a lot of pain and mad as hell, I threw the device at them and drove to my apartment for first aid. I still have the scar on my chest from that mishap that could have gotten me hurt.

Near the end of the investigation, Mickey had a feeling that there was a rat in his crew. He was right, it was me. Early one morning he called us to the social club, just to shake us up and maybe find out who the mole was. He barked that if there was an informer working among us, he would eventually ferret him out and deal with him in his own way. We knew what he meant. I became a pro at hiding my feelings, but it took its toll, feeling like an armature that was being wound up so tight that it was about to explode.

Mickey's drug dealing was going to put him away for the rest of his life. The investigation was wrapping up soon and the thought of Mickey's future, put a shiver up my spine. I was putting an end to the life he knew. I was responsible for taking away his freedom, even if he deserved it. Arrest and search warrants were about to be executed any day. Just thinking about it kept me awake at night. I'd lay there in the early morning hours, in that dump of an apartment, thinking about how things were going to shake out. My fucking mind just wouldn't shut off and my heart rate would accelerate to the point where I thought I was going to stroke out. Many nights I had to drink myself to sleep and pay the price of a hangover the next day. I worried that I might not be able to assimilate back into a normal life after this was over. What would I be doing on my job? Would I be able to adjust back into the squad? My concerns upset the hell out of me. During this whole ordeal,

I'd lost my wife and kids and that cut deep into my soul. I've been working with the mob for so long, it totally changed who I was. I was an island unto myself without any sense of compassion for people left.

How could I be living a double life and it not have affected me? I wondered if my bosses thought about me coming back into the squad and how I would adjust? Nothing was ever mentioned. I wondered if they gave a damn. I had worries about reacquainting myself with my kids. And of course, there was my mom, dad and brother Rich. I've been out of touch with my family for so long, we needed to reconnect. Would they understand? But how could they really understand what it's like to lead a double life, not knowing who the good guys are and who the bad guys are supposed to be? I locked away a special place in my mind to protect who I was before I went deep undercover. I wondered if I could unlock that part of me that I hid for so long and find myself.

Now it was just a matter of days before Mickey and the crew were going to be arrested. I was a nervous wreck for it to be over. I hadn't cleaned my apartment in weeks, anticipating finally getting out of that shit-hole. A few times Mickey told me to clean the place up. It was a disgrace, he lamented. He didn't want to set foot in the apartment until it was cleaned. The trash cans in the living room and kitchen were overflowing with empty beer cans and liquor bottles. All the ashtrays were full of burnt butts, left by the degenerates who visited me. Dirty pans on the stove and the dishes on the kitchen table were scattered alongside empty pizza boxes. Laughing to myself, I thought, he'd never have to set foot in here again. He was going to prison for a long time.

When it was all over, it was like having a 100-pound weight lifted off of my shoulders. I was so excited about getting my life back, but still uncertain of the outcome. The plan was to flip Mickey and have him testify against the higher-ups in his crime family. He was offered a deal. If he cooperated, he would do very little jail time, that was the hook. He and his family would be given a new identity and placed into the witness protection program. Detectives from my office grilled Mickey in our interrogation room for hours on end. He repeatedly asked to speak to his lawyer and was adamant that he didn't want to cooperate with the government.

It must have been after midnight when Chief Daniels had squad Detective Ron Sidney call me on my cell. "Frank, the chief wants to see you in his office right away." At the time, I was resting on one of the bunk beds in the locker room, trying my best to get my head together. Ron, a cop's cop, was a good friend and I trusted him to watch my back. He'd always be there for me when I needed him. Ron, tall, muscular, hazel eyed and fair skinned was always well groomed. I referred to him as Mr. GQ. He immigrated from Wales not long after college and then he brought his wife and kids over.

"Ron, tell the chief I'm on my way."

When I walked into the chief's office, he was standing in front of his desk popping Pepto Bismol tablets into his mouth. I guess he was suffering from nerves from pressure caused from the Calise take down. Besides his stomach trouble, he was his usual unemotional self. There was no hello Frank, nice job. How are you holding up? There was no, you must be relieved it's over. There was none of that. The first thing that the son of a bitch asked was, "Frank, where is your shield?"

"It's right here in my pocket Chief."

"You know that we have Mickey in the interrogation room. He's clammed up and far as we can tell, he doesn't know that you're a cop yet. I wanted you to go in there and tell him who you are. That may shock him into cooperating."

I felt like the prick just hit me over the head with a two-by-four. I wasn't prepared mentally to walk into the interrogation room and tell Mickey that I'm a cop and ask him to cooperate. This is the guy that wanted me to marry his daughter. This is the same guy who took me under his wing in his criminal world, as crazy as it sounds, he's the guy who told me that every other guy works for the FBI and to be careful who I trust. My stomach was churning. I could taste the bile in my mouth. It was like scraping off little pieces of my soul, bit by bit. At the very least, the Chief should have known how hard that would be for me, but he didn't give a shit. The self-inflated egotist only cared about himself and his career. He didn't care that my marriage was over and I had no relationship with my kids. Asking me to walk in and tell Mickey that I was cop; wanting him to become a rat was outrageous. I knew Mickey and what he was made of. I knew without a doubt that he'd never flip.

The minute I walked into the interrogation room, Mickey's face lit up. He was sitting at a small wooden table fumbling nervously with his hands that were handcuffed to the table. The first thing he said was, "Cheech, they got you too." I didn't say anything, emotionless, I just looked at him. I reached into my jeans and pulled out a black leather case holding my police shield and identification card. I threw them on the table in front of him. Mickey stared at them for a moment and cringed. His face began to contort. He then opened his mouth and bit through his tongue. He gave out a loud moan. Blood began to stream from his mouth and drip down onto his polo shirt and he shook uncontrollably. I stood there frozen in front of him, I was freaked out too. Trying to get a grip on the situation, I finally said, "Mickey, my office wants your cooperation. They want information about the higher-ups in the family. For your testimony, they'll set you up in a new life. You'll be able to start over."

Mickey, continued to tremble and stare at my identification, shaking his head as he tried to compose himself, he took a short pause and said, "Cheech, I can't do that. They'll find me and kill me and my family. Now please go."

I stormed out of the room, pushing passed the chief and headed for the squad room. I didn't have to tell them what Mickey's reply was, they knew. The room was wired for sound, the conversation was also videoed and the room has a two-way mirrored wall. I wasn't in the squad room but for a few minutes when one of the typists approached me.

"Frank, can I ask you a question."

"Sure Marge, what is it?"

She looked directly at me and said, "Frank, don't you feel like a rat?" Marge nearly knocked me off my feet by her question. Regaining my balance, I stared through her for a second, dumbfounded. I couldn't believe she asked me that. She worked for a law enforcement agency and was vetted. I answered her sharply. "No Marge, I don't feel like a rat. I'm a cop!" I walked away in a demoralized state.

I took some time off from work. I had to. I couldn't go right back; I had to get myself together and find out who I was. What happened to me next was a physiological cluster fuck. I was unable to speak for weeks. The words just wouldn't come out of my mouth, even when I tried to force them out. All the years of working for the syndicate and the stress it created was bottled up inside of me. I felt like a volcano that was about to explode. The only thing that seemed to help was spending time in the Bronx Botanical Garden. I needed to be alone, it was peaceful. After a while I began to let go of some of the pent-up anger, negative feelings and frustration swirling around in my mind. Finally, I got a sense of who I am, who I was meant to be. I'm an undercover cop. I did a job and I'd have to deal with everything that came along with it. I was ready to get my life back.

Chapter Twelve

Reentry into the DA's Detective division would take some time getting used to. As I've already mentioned, the Chief reassigned me to the narcotics squad where he felt that I could be of most use. His ulterior motive, he always had one, was that I would make good press for the office.

One of the major tools that law enforcement has is the use of informants. Developing a working relationship with informers is no easy task. There are many obstacles involved in growing a good working relationship, not to mention that it's complicated and dangerous. The C.I. (Confidential Informant) has to develop a trust with the cop he's working with. The trust doesn't happen overnight. It happens over a period of time, trial and error. Each informant is unique with many idiosyncrasies. It's up to the undercover to figure out the person's peculiarities and work with them, if they are going have any kind of success. The informant needs to feel that the police officer is working in his/her best interests to keep them safe and out of jail. One of the pitfalls with working with an informant, at least it was for me, was the double dealing, or in layman's terms, selling you out to the other side. Their plan, that is the C.I and drug dealer, is to pocket the buy money and kill the cop. Many cops have been shot and killed as well as drug dealers in this exchange. In the back of my mind, I knew that I could never totally trust any informant. But they are a necessary evil. It's safer for a narcotics officer to make a case on his own. However more often than not, most of my cases were made through an informant who made the initial contact with the drug dealer. Playing the role of a narcotics trafficker, looking for a new source of product is an arduous task. The drug dealers I had to deal with eroded away any sense of decency I might have felt for them.

The way I conducted business was to have my C.I. start by making low level narcotic buys and work his or her way up the food chain. When they got far enough up in the chain, I'd have them introduce me as a connected guy with ties to the mob. I always felt that low level dealers were victims themselves and only dealt drugs to support their own addiction. Many times, I turned a blind eye when it came to locking up the low-level dealers. Personally, I was only interested in targeting the major narcotic suppliers who imported the poison into our country, killing thousands of people each year. A major turning point in my career was when I was assigned to work with a federal informant whose family was involved in bringing heroin into the country from the Middle East. The guy was a Jordanian American who had been convicted at trial with the other members in his family. He was sentenced to ten years in federal prison, but rather than do his time, he decided to work his beef off. He signed on as a C.I., working for the US Attorney's Office. By making major narcotics cases, it would lessen the time he'd have to spend in prison.

His name is Ayman Baraka. In Arabic, Ayman translates to Mike or Michael in English. He could easily pass for an Italian American. In fact, when we first met in the U.S. Attorney's Office, I thought that he was of Italian descent. As the ladies say, he's tall dark and handsome. Baraka measures six-feet tall, well built, dark brown eyes, black hair, slicked back and is a smooth talker. All the ladies love him because he is so personable and charming. I marveled how easy it was for him to talk to people, especially, women. I wish it was that easy for me, it's not. I figured that Mike, who he likes to be called, was the guy who could make me shine again in my department.

Ayman, from the get-go, maintained his innocence. Almost every informant I've ever worked with said that they were innocent of the crime they were convicted of. We know that the criminal justice system has some flaws, some people are innocent and have been sent to prison unjustly. Ayman was one of them, but that's for later.

I had a lot on my plate during this time in my life. I had to finally face the fact that I was divorced and living alone. I'll admit it, I cried myself to sleep most nights that I wasn't drunk. But this was the hand that I was dealt and I had to plod along with my life. As I mentioned earlier, I had to believe in my undercover persona. I had to reinforce that I was Frank Miranda and not Frank Santorsola, an undercover cop. I needed the drug dealers to believe that I was a half-ass wise guy looking to score narcotics. I dressed the part, with all the bling. The feds even gave me a Mercedes Benz S550 to drive and to change things up, a Porsche 911. What kept me afloat during this time was spending quality time with mom and dad. There were dinners out with my brother and Sunday dinners at my mom's house. This made my transition back into the squad a lot easier.

Not long after our traditional get together at my folk's house, we were at his bedside in the intensive care unit at New York Columbia Presbyterian Hospital, in Manhattan. He suffered a massive heart attack and soon passed away. In that stark hospital room, there was an overwhelming feeling of emptiness that took hold of me, thinking of living in a world without him. Like I said, he was our guide, counselor, our rock of Gibraltar, our father. Death is so final and that is so hard to face when someone you love dies. The reality of it is that we'll never see or speak to him again.

Chapter Thirteen

There are a few benefits working undercover. One of them is driving high end cars that don't have cop written all over them. Depending on the target of the investigation, I had a number of expensive cars at my disposal. The cars had been seized from drug dealers during prior narcotic investigations. The office also paid for an apartment in the Bronx. It was rented using my undercover identity.

The first few times out with Baraka, I worked with my newly assigned partner, Joe Nulligan. Right from the beginning, Baraka and Joe were like oil and water. You didn't have to be Einstein to see that they just didn't get along. Joe, in his late thirties, is a redhead, has deep-set blue eyes and is built like a brick shit-house. He'd rather run head on through a problem than calmly deal with it. When we first started working with Mike, we'd cruise the streets, sometimes pulling to the curb, and more often not, double parking, watching actual buys go down. But in reality, the only thing that I was focused on was getting a read on Mike; trying to see where the guy was coming from and if he had the balls to make narcotic cases and keep me in action.

Like me, Joe was burnt out. He'd been working in the trenches so long that he couldn't hide his negative feelings, especially when it came to dealing with informants. From the jump, he treated Baraka abrasively and was contemptuous of him. I immediately saw that the marriage between them wasn't going to work. Me on the other hand, I still wanted to make cases. Baraka seemed bright and had a huge incentive to stay out of jail. As I mentioned he and his family were convicted of importing heroin from the Middle East, so he had to know the right people to connect with.

It was just a matter of time before the shit hit the fan. One night, Joe got in Baraka's face and got physical with him. For some reason, Joe flew off the handle and exploded. He grabbed Baraka by the throat and forced him to the ground. Mike pushed himself up, brushed the dirt off and said bitterly, "Frank, this isn't gonna work. Keep that fuck away from me. Take me home."

In the back of my mind my intuition was telling me that Mike was going to call his lawyer and complain about Joe. Sure enough, Mike's lawyer, Joan Connolly, a former federal prosecutor, demanded that Nulligan have no further contact with her client. Connolly, who I met earlier in the US Attorney's Office, is in her early forties, very sexy and a petite woman. She dresses in a conservative manner, but I have a feeling underneath it all, she's a passionate woman, waiting for someone to unharness her stifled sexual desire.

Connolly was adamant, if her client was to continue to work with my office, he would only work with me. This was not according to protocol. There were important issues to consider. I'd be working without a partner and if there was an integrity situation it would be my word against Baraka's. However, I had little say in the matter and it had been decided by the DA, Joe would be reassigned and I'd be working without a partner.

I had no partner or back-up when I worked in Calise's street crew. I know what it feels like to be out there on my own, it's a dangerous place to be. The fact of the matter is that I'm just getting over the trauma that the Calise investigation had on me and my personal life.

Working narcotics cases without a partner is unusual, but deep down I knew I could handle it. I've gotten accustomed to working alone and as crazy as it sounds, I liked it. The only person that I was really responsible for was me and I could run the cases like I wanted to. The downside of it all is that I don't know Baraka from Adam and narcotics is a dirty business. Most narc's get a reputation of taking money. There's a lot of money involved in narcotic trafficking and the conjecture is that you're dirty and on the take.

I'm not saying that it would happen, but Mike could accuse me of pocketing money from one of the drug dealers. Without a partner, it'll be his and his lawyer's word against mine. I took this into account and I figured if I want to advance my career, Mike could be my ticket for a promotion. I'd just have to keep a close eye on him and see to it that he walks the straight and narrow. If he tries to jam me up in any way, I'll pull the plug on him so fast he'd be back in the slam before he knew what hit him. As I said, I'm just barely getting over the years I spent working for Mickey. I'll have to muster all the energy I have and make sure that everything goes according to Hoyle. The upside is of all of this if the cases go well, I'll be on the fast track to advance in rank. In any event, I'd just have to monitor Mike closely and make sure he doesn't do anything stupid.

As far as the Chief and the DA were concerned, they were only interested in making it into the media. The Chief worked at the pleasure of the DA and he had to keep her happy. DA Larson is a politician in every sense of the word. She's petite, in her mid-forties, chic in her manor of dress and extremely bright and calculating. She's betting that me and Baraka will keep her and her office in the spotlight on a regular basis. Like I said, I can size a person up in an instant and Larson was no exception. If I couldn't help Annette Larson advance her agenda, I'd be just another burnt out cop that she'll discard on her rise to power.

I was given everything I needed to play the role of a mobbed-up guy. I had a bankroll to buy clothes and imported Italian shoes, a diamond pinky ring and an 18-carat gold chain with two dice that hung off the end. If I'm going to play the role of a mobster, I had to look and feel the part. After all, I was pretending to be one of them for years.

So, it's me and Baraka. I was hoping that he could connect with some major importers and soon. I didn't let on to my bosses that I was excited about working with Mike. If the Chief finally figured out that I got an adrenaline high from living on the edge, he'd expect far more from me. I wish I knew why I loved living in the fast lane, but I truly don't. Maybe I love the uncertainty of the danger that comes with making deals with drug dealers and wise guys. Or perhaps, I just love the risk of it all. I know one thing for certain, I don't like taking orders and I like making my own decisions. If anything goes wrong, I only have myself to blame.

Ever since I met Baraka, he's been telling me that it was his look-alike cousin, Ayman Hanni, conspired with Calise to distribute heroin and not him. He said that he'd been railroaded by the government and that the law enforcement agencies involved in the investigation dropped the ball. They didn't take the time to differentiate the two and got the wrong guy. I wondered if Baraka was telling the truth. At any rate, I'd soon find out. If he was, I frankly couldn't see how he could connect with major drug dealers since, according to him, he had no dealings with them.

Chapter Fourteen

As unusual as it might sound, I was comfortable in places where the lower stratum of society and the bottom feeders hung out. I'd frequent these bat and ball joints and so-called restaurants to keep my persona sharp, a knock around street guy. I'd converse with strangers at the bar, while sipping on a scotch from a tumbler and getting the beat of what's going on in the street. Our conversation might revolve around the New York Yankees game, what the odds are on the next New York Giants football game or what the local shy-lock's interest rates are, all along convincing them I was one of them.

There was this bar/restaurant called Goomba Johnny's on Bronxdale Avenue in the Bronx, where I hung out. The Italian food was great and the portions large. Before every major narcotic buy, I'd have lunch there to get my head in the right place. I have to laugh, one day I was parking my car in front of the restaurant and a black Mercedes-Benz pulled up, parking in front of me. I recognized the driver as a professional baseball player who plays for one of the New York teams. If I mentioned his name, you'd know him. He got out of the car along with another guy. Once on the sidewalk, the pro baseball player grabbed the guy by his arm and forcefully grabbed him. They were face to face. He then hauled off and bitch slapped the guy across his face, knocking him to the sidewalk. He hit him so hard I heard the slap from the inside my car. He's African American, 6' 5", 250 pounds and shaves his head. Now his so-called friend is lying on the ground for a few seconds, when the pro baseball player bends down and pulled the guy to his feet, brushing the dirt off him, takes him by the arm and walked him into the restaurant. A minute or so later, I walked in and sat down in a booth behind them. They were chatting and acting like nothing had happened. Go figure! Now I happen to be a Met fan and I couldn't help myself, I got up walked over and asked the outfielder for his autograph. He smiled, signing his name on the back of a match cover that I slid in front of him. I still can't figure out what the problem between them was, but it reinforced the old adage, expect the unexpected.

I'd pick up some good intelligence by hanging around in places like this, sometimes my information would lead to other investigations. A noted wise guy, who trafficked in narcotics, frequented Goomba Johnny's on a regular basis. I walked into the restaurant one late afternoon and overheard him talking about receiving a package of cocaine. I heard him say he'd meet the person in front of the restaurant at noon the next day. As a result of his cell call to discuss drug trafficking, my office and the DEA Task Force had probable cause to have a judge sign an eavesdropping warrant and place a tap on the guy's phone. The wire lasted a few months and the wise guy along with other traffickers were subsequently arrested and prosecuted. A large quantity of drugs and money were seized in the process. This is how things happen in my world, they just seem to fall into my lap.

Another low-life establishment I spent a lot of time in to hone my skills was The Melody Club. It's a strip club on the Yonkers/Bronx border. Girls danced nude around a steel pole, under an overhead jeweled disco ball. Wise guys spent big bucks for lap dances and other sorted sexual favors from the strippers. Stevie H. was one of them. Stevie ran a sports book for John Iacone, a half-ass wise guy. We'd occasionally run into one another and soon became friends. We spent many late nights at the bar, drinking, shooting the shit about his sports book and patronizing the girls for lap dances.

That's where I first met Denise Mackenzie. At five feet eight, long shiny blond hair, bright green eyes and a shapely body, the girl is a knockout. She wasn't like the other girls; never taking her G-string off and as she told me, she only stripped to pay her college tuition. At the time, as far as she knew I was a wise guy like the other guys. For some reason she was attracted to me. I noticed her flirtatious looks as she strutted her wears on stage. At times during her breaks, she'd come over and we'd talk. It wasn't long before we were comfortable with one another. We felt an instant connection. Denise was different, she seemed to be grounded. Her goal was to complete her Master's Degree in geology at Columbia University and move on. The Melody Club afforded her the means to pay her tuition, rent and other living expenses. To this day I ask myself why she was attracted to me. She told me once that she's a good judge of character and "Besides" she said, "you look like Tom Selleck and I love him." Hey, the girl is gorgeous and it was about time to get back into the dating game even though my heart wasn't completely healed. I still missed Helen and the kids terribly. Although I knew Denise for several months, I still wasn't ready to tell her that I was a cop. I didn't fully trust her and didn't know if she was friendly with any of the wise guys who patronized the club. I couldn't take a chance that she might tell them that I was a cop. We'd have to let our relationship play out and see where it went.

Getting back to Stevie, like I said, he ran sports book for John Iacone out of an apartment in the North Bronx on Carpenter Avenue. NYPD's Vice Enforcement Unit and detectives from my office raided his wire room. Stevie was charged with promoting and possessing gambling records in the 1st degree. The crimes are non-violent, so a low bail was set and he was let out pending the adjudication of the charges. The only problem Stevie had was that he was a predicate felon, (repeat offender) and by New York State law had to do 1 ½ to 3 years in the state pen. I knew Stevie and he wasn't the type of guy who could stand up for himself in prison. He told me during our many conversations that the only downside to the life he was leading was going to prison. It terrified him.

La Cosa Nostra, which means, our thing, have sources in the law enforcement community. It's amazing what money will buy. Some people, including cops have no self-respect for themselves or the oath of office they took. Somehow, someway, it got back to Iacone that Stevie might be cooperating with the FBI. Unfortunately, that sealed his fate. Whether or not he was cooperating is a moot point. He was found shot to death in one of the parking lots at Kennedy Airport. His body was stuffed into the trunk of his car. A passerby smelled the stench of his decomposing body coming from the trunk. Knowing Stevie and knowing how he ended up, haunts me to this day. He was shot like a dog and disposed of like trash. The movies somehow glamorized these guys as folk heroes. They are brutal killers with no regard for human life and shouldn't be allowed to walk among us.

Chapter Fifteen

Mike Baraka developed his first lead. His name was Hector Cruz, a mid-level cocaine dealer who worked directly for the Medellin Cartel in Columbia. At the time, the cartel was highly organized, originating from the city of Medellin. It was headed by Pablo Escobar. Escobar was a much feared and ruthless drug lord. It's said that he is responsible for countless murders of Mexican police officers, politicians and civilians. He has since met his end at the hands of the Colombian National Police.

Cruz was a dangerous man with tentacles reaching directly to Escobar. He'd kill you in a heartbeat if he suspected that you were an informer or cop. The concern I had was that Cruz not find out who Mike and I are until he's taken off the street. We'd be screwed if he found out and everybody connected to us would be in harm's way. Several thoughts crossed my mind as I contemplated meeting Cruz. I needed to know this guy inside and out and I had to have total control of the field operation. My life and Mike's life depended on it.

At times, I wished I was able to settle for mundane police work, but I can't. Then again, there isn't any such thing as routine police work, it's all dangerous. A county parkway cop I knew, stopped a car on a routine traffic stop. The guy driving the car was wanted for a double murder in upstate New York. When Felix asked to see the guy's license and registration, Felix was shot dead. The animal that killed him was killed a week later in a police shoot out. So like I said, there's nothing routine in police work. I thrive on the excitement of pushing the envelope with the bad-est of the bad. I needed another adrenaline fix to motivate me and Hector Cruz was gonna give it to me. It ain't rocket science. I know what I gotta do. I have to convince Cruz that I'm Frank Miranda, a connected guy, looking for a new supplier of cocaine.

I'm thinking that there must be much more to Baraka than meets the eye. He's bringing me Cruz, maybe he isn't the innocent man he claims to be. Like any informant, my instincts were not to trust him. Most are on drugs, self-medicating, and after all Baraka's only working with me to stay out of jail. Mike found out that Cruz was a regular at the Red Rooster Lounge, a shit buck dive in South Yonkers. There have been more than a few knifing and shootings in the joint.

Everyone has their peculiarities and superstitions, I'm no exception. Mine revolved around a brown suit. It is medium-weight, worsted wool for any season. I wore this suit on all undercover jobs that had hair on it. What I mean is when I didn't have full control of a dangerous situation. I felt and believed that the suit would keep me safe and it hasn't failed me. I haven't received a scratch since I began to wear it and I planned to continue to wear it until I retired. I'd never wear it for mundane activities like trying to impress a girl on a date, it might spoil the karma.

That night I decided not to request backup, but I'm rolling the dice. Hector would have his people around, that's a given. I suspected that they were in the bar with eyes on us, looking for anything suspicious. If Hector or his people spotted cops in the area, that would definitely queer the deal and Hector Cruz would be, as they say, in the wind. I knew that the chief and my squad commander would be pissed at me for not having cops on the set to watch my back. If anything happened to me or the informant, their careers would be over.

I couldn't help but rub my lucky brown suit when I walked into the Red Rooster Lounge. I was finally meeting Hector Cruz. For me, it felt like a pro football player on the field waiting for the whistle to blow to start the game. If Cruz turned out to be the real deal, it would be a very interesting night. Little did I know how interesting it would be.

The bar was dimly lit, crowded and three rows deep. The bartender, Chester Doolittle, looked like something out of Barnum and Bailey Circus. He was approximately forty, weighted about 300 pounds, stood 5' 4" tall and completely bald. The red florescent light in the shape of a red rooster hung behind the bar and lit up his head shinny head like the reflection of a traffic light on a wet street. Chester wore creamed colored slacks pulled up above his waist and held up by bright red suspenders.

I pushed my way through the crowded bar and noticed Mike sitting in the dining room. Baraka was casually dressed, wore jeans, a green polo shirt and a light brown leather jacket. I could tell by his body language that he was nervous. I told him to calm down before Hector got here. I didn't let on that I was nervous too.

The waitress, a middle aged, dyed blonde, buxom woman showing a little too much cleavage and a lot of life's wear, came over and asked what we wanted a drink. "I'll have a Dewar's on the rocks." Mike ordered a Budweiser. She returned with the drinks in short order.

It must have been a little after ten when Hector walked in. He looked like something out of a John Shaft movie. The dude wore a gray jogging suit, designer sneakers and a large gold chain around his neck. He walked over and Mike introduced me. Hector made it a point to sit directly across from me to study my body language, looking for the slightest hint that I wasn't who I said I was. What he didn't know was that I was poring over every inch of him too. I wanted this buy to happen. It would mean a feather in my cap and my bosses would have less fodder to use to reprimanded me for not having backup. The waitress returned with a rum and coke for Hector. She definitely knew him and what he drank. After making small talk for several minutes, Hector stood and said, "Amigo call me in an hour I have something for you." He threw $100 on the table and walked out. Well, I thought the evening isn't over yet.

What happened next would put a lasting scare in my brain. An hour passed and it was time to call Hector. He asked me to meet him at Post and Lexington Avenue in Yonkers, about a ten-minute ride. It was after eleven when I pulled onto Lexington Avenue. On one side of the avenue is an industrial park and the other side was lined with rundown tenements. I figured that Cruz had his guys on the street and that made me feel uneasy. As I drove up the block, I spotted Hector standing on the corner, he was waving me over. I reached down under the driver's seat and stuck my 357 into my waist, then Mike and I got out of the car. With his hand in the air, he motioned and shouted, "Only you Frank! My gift is only for you!" Hector then walked out into the center of the intersection and stood under a blinking yellow streetlight. At the time, I can honestly say that I wasn't thinking about anything, I was just reacting to the situation. I could feel that my senses were in tune with my surroundings. I heard the muted crackling of the halogen street lights as the electric current flowed through them. Suddenly, I felt constriction in my stomach and had to control my breathing. I could hear my heart pounding in my ears. The reality of the situation had finally sunken in and the thought shot through my mind that this might not go well tonight. Maybe I was in over my head and should have called for backup. I wished I was any place but here. I hoped that Cruz didn't hear my damn knees rattling as I approached him. He looked up and down the street to make sure I came alone. We were now face to face, he grinned, his gold teeth shimmered from the reflection of the florescent streetlights. With one hand he pulled out a small tin foil packet from his jumpsuit pocket and simultaneously drew a 25 caliber semi-automatic pistol with his other, pushing it into my forehead. His forefinger was resting on the trigger, he handed me the tin foil packet and demanded that I open it. My eyes were riveted on the pistol as I slowly opened the packet of white powdery substance. Hector bellowed, "Take a taste!" My mind raced, as the acid shot up from my stomach into my mouth. I was on the verge of getting physically sick. I had to control my mind and body, I had no choice. I had to pretend to snort the shit or I was a dead man. At that very moment, I could see my life flash before my eyes, kissing everyone I loved and saying my goodbyes.

I slowly unfolded the tinfoil and removed a small amount of the white powder, placing it on my left palm and with the other hand I sealed the packet and put it into my jacket pocket, it was evidence. I had to think fast. Should I go for my gun and shoot the son of a bitch and get it over with or pretend to snort it? Snorting it was the most logical option. I cautiously turned away from Cruz and bent over, taking a pinch of the substance, rubbed it onto my right nostril and blocked the nostril with my finger. I then inhaled deeply through the other nostril. After shivering for effect, I prayed he bought my bit. I turned back towards him and looked him dead in the eye. He obviously saw the ring of powder left around my right nostril. Studying me for a moment, he lunged forward, and grabbed me in a bear hug, the silver pistol still in his hand. I was a blithering basket case. I'd almost pissed myself, but Hector bought my act and was now in my back pocket. Before we walked away from one another, Hector was all set to sell me a few kilos of coke as a starter. I won the game that night, but the mental toll was mind blowing.

Chapter Sixteen

The fact of the matter is, everything I did was dangerous. I had something pop up while I waited for Cruz to contact me. I met Jose Colon in a bar on Morris Park Avenue in the Bronx and we struck up a conversation that led to his gun trafficking. He was a 25-year-old street punk, illegally here from Mexico. We scheduled to meet the next day on the service road of the Major Deegan Expressway, near 233rd Street in the Bronx. Like clockwork, the dirt bag showed up and parked his old beat-up Chevy Impala behind my car. He climbed into my back seat carrying a large brown paper bag. Jose was dressed in jeans and a sweatshirt and was nervous as hell. "You got money?" he snapped.

Turning slightly around so I could see him, I replied, "Yeah, I got money, let's see what you got."

Jose dumped the bag containing several pistols on the back seat and pointed to the assorted guns. "Frank, how many do you want?"

"You spoke about $350.00 a gun. I had no idea you had all these to sell. I'd brought more money."

I looked over the arsenal of weapons. There was a 380 Sig Sauer, a 9 mm Smith & Wesson, a 380 Hechler & Koch, a snub nose 38 Colt revolver and a 9mm Glock semi-automatic pistol. I was amazed. I knew these guns were stolen, they had to be. Without a doubt they'd end up in the wrong hands and most likely be used in the commission of a violent crime. I needed to get him and the guns off the street. The unfortunate thing was that I only had $1,000.00 on me. If I had more money, I'd buy the lot of them. As I was thinking that I should lock the bastard up then and there, I felt the barrel of a gun up against my head. My heart almost stopped beating. Jose leaned forward and with a menacing and piercing stare, growled, "I'll take everything in your wallet, my friend."

I slowly removed my wallet while Jose held the pistol to my head. He snatched the wallet from my hand, peeled out $1,000 in $50 and $100 bills and flung the wallet in my face. The bum then took his time putting the guns back into the bag and split. I should have suspected that he never intended to sell me a gun by the way he was acting. I sat there for a moment mulling over what just happened. I was lucky that the cocksucker didn't pull the trigger. Again, I didn't have backup. If I had backup, Jose would have ended up in the can.

As they say, payback is a bitch. I caught up with him a few months later. I found out from an informant that he worked as a stock boy in a local supermarket in South Yonkers. One afternoon, Joe Nulligan and I walked into the supermarket and found him stocking shelves with canned goods. He was crouched down, placing cans of vegetables on the lower shelf. Joe and I approached him quietly, with guns drawn. The little weasel was distracted and didn't hear us come up behind him. Now it was my turn the make the little shit squirm. I banged my 357 up against the back of his head and shouted, "Remember me motherfucker! You're under arrest!" He turned his head slowly and looked at me. "Surprise, surprise, asshole!" I yelled. His eyes were as wide as silver dollars. He panicked and went for a box cutter that he had in his pants pocket, but it was too late. Nulligan reacted like only Joe could. He hit him on the side of his head with the butt of his gun, rendering the punk unconscious. I put the handcuffs on him as tight as they would ratchet up. I made him feel the pain as he grimaced and yelled ouch! We then dragged the little prick out of the store, like a side of beef and threw him in the back of Joe's Crown Victoria, whisking him off to jail. After doing some hard time for grand larceny, assaulting a police officer and firearms trafficking, Jose was turned over to the Immigration and Nationalization service and deported back to Mexico.

Unfortunately for me, my lucky brown suit couldn't help me with my personal demons. I was drinking way too much and couldn't hide it from anyone. I really think that my department should have gotten me help but didn't. The pressures of undercover life were immense. Drinking became a daily routine and I looked forward to it. It was an escape valve. I had some relief, if only for a few hours.

Chapter Seventeen

As I look back on some of my most difficult, but satisfying investigations in my career, they have come back to life again in writing this book. The one thing that has stayed with me throughout my professional life is that many police officers think that guys like me, who worked narcotic investigation, have taken money along the way. No question about it, narcotic traffickers can make a great deal of money. So for narcs, there's always the temptation to steal drugs or money. I guess some narcotic investigators feel that the money is ill gotten and won't be missed by anyone, so why not help yourself to some. But I've seen it, it catches up to you at some point in your career and it's not a happy ending for the police officer. Pensions are lost and lives are ruined, it's never worth it.

I was once told by one of my bosses that eventually a narcotic cop, if he stays in the game long enough, will become dirty. His reasoning was that most cops barely scrape y on their police salary. A lot are divorced, paying alimony and child support. The temptation for easy money is hard to resist. I remember how hard it was when I was paying alimony and child support. At the time, I had only enough money to buy canned food for lunch and dinner. Forget about eating out or taking in a movie when you're left with only a few dollars in your pocket after each paycheck. I finally saw financial daylight when my ex-wife remarried and I didn't have to pay alimony any longer. So for some cops, the sight of hundreds of thousands of dollars of confiscated drug money staring you in the face is hard to resist. Taking some is a quick fix to their financial problems. I gotta thank my father for literally beating it into my head that anyone who is capable of stealing a penny, is capable of thievery, period. The sky's the limit!

One of the more routine narcotic cases I was involved in had to do with search warrants for a drug dealer's two-bedroom apartment and his vehicle. There were approximately ten cops assigned to the detail, me being one of them. After the knucklehead's door was knocked off its hinges with a 20 lb steel battering ram, the warrants were executed and the apartment was secured for the officers safety. I was assigned to search the druggies old beat-up red Volkswagen, parked in the tenant's parking lot. I got down to the parking lot to find that the Volkswagen was the only car in the lot. The car's body was rusted and dented. After rummaging through the interior and finding nothing, I moved to the trunk, expecting it to be locked. To my surprise, there was a hole where the trunk lock used to be. I lifted the trunk, which was positioned in the front of the car and to my utter amazement, it was filled from front to back with money in denominations of $5.00, $10.00 and $20.00 bills. The first thing that came to mind was that I didn't want to be accused of taking any of the money by drug dealer or the cops. At the top of my lungs, screaming into the portable radio, I yelled for a superior to get down here. Within a matter of minutes Sgt. Mercurio came running out of the building and into the lot. "What's the problem Frankie? Are you okay?"

"The trunk is loaded with money! Have someone photograph it and it has to be counted!"

Sgt. Mercurio's eyes almost popped out of his head as he gazed on all that money. On his portable, he yelled for detectives Ron Sidney and Ken, *Boom Boom* DeGrossi to get down to the parking lot and to bring the camera!" Ken got the handle Boom Boom because he shoots first and asks questions later.

The trunk was photographed by Boom Boom and the money was painstakingly counted by Detective Ron. It ended up that the trunk held $1,500,000 in small bills. Gees, talk about temptation. The sight of all that money definitely separated the honest from the corrupt.

Fast forward to confidential informant Mike (Ayman) Baraka and his issues of honor and trust. After the touch-and-go meeting on Lexington Street with Hector Cruz, we headed back to the Red Rooster Lounge so Mike could pick up his car. It began to rain heavily. Making our way onto the Sawmill River Parkway and exiting at Palmer Avenue, Mike seemed to have settled down from the drama that just occurred between me and Cruz just moments ago and blurted out, "Frank, I have some information you might be interested in."

My juices were still pumping from the exchange with Cruz and my mind was on overdrive. I couldn't imagine what he had to say. "What Mike? What's so important it can't wait?"

Mike's gaze was fixated on the road ahead. "Look, I know of an Arab who a transports half million in drug money, twice a week to Washington D.C. I know the route he takes."

I sat up, gripping the steering wheel tightly, wondering why he hasn't mentioned this before? "Who's he working for?"

Glancing at me for a moment, then looking back out of the front windshield he replied, "A heroin dealer named Khalid Asar. He's a meek guy and he never carries a gun. I was thinking, we could stop him, you could flash your badge and we take the money and leave. No one has to know."

Mike had just crossed the line and I was fuming. Maybe he thought I might take the bait. I never thought to check him for a wire, the FBI could be listening in. I turned the wheel hard, turning onto the shoulder and slamming on the brakes. In a flash, I was out of the car and yanked him out of the car by his shirt collar, shouting, "You just committed the cardinal sin, motherfucker!" I knocked him to the ground and dragged him out to the center of Palmer Avenue. With one hand on his shoulders, pinning him to the road, my other hand held his head to the asphalt, "You see that fucking yellow line?" I yelled. "Take a good look at it. I'm that double yellow line, I don't go to the right of it or to the left of it! You freakin' got it! I don't take money, period!"

Infuriated, I kept his head pressed to the road and growled, "Are you wearing a wire?"

"No, no! I'm not wired! I swear!"

"If I ever hear anything like that come out of your mouth again, I'll pull the plug so fast you'll be back in the slam before you blink your eyes twice. Do you understand what I'm saying? Now get back in the car."

Mike still trembling, brushed himself off as he walked back to the car and said, "Frank, I just needed to know where you're coming from. I made the story up. I need to be able to trust you. Right now, I don't know who to trust."

Continuing our ride to The Red Rooster Lounge to get his car, I told him that trusting me wasn't his main problem. After what he just pulled, his concern should be whether or not I'm still willing to work with him. "Remember Mike, trust goes both ways."

Chapter Eighteen

Trust is a word that at times is used too loosely. For the most part, it's faith or belief in something or someone. Do I trust my brother? Absolutely. Do I trust Joe Nulligan? I trust Joe with my life. Do I trust Denise MacKenzie? Well, something happened when we first started to date that gave me an insight into her character and what she's made of, but do I trust her yet? I don't know.

It was a cold day in January and I was off for the weekend. Denise and I decided to get way and try our hand at skiing. We rented a chalet near one of the ski resorts in the Pocono Mountains of Pennsylvania, about a two-hour ride from New York City. I'd rented this chalet before, knew the owner and knew the area like the back of my hand. After we arrived and settled in, we headed for the slopes which was only a mile or two away. On the ride to the ski resort, I suddenly lost perspective of where I was, began to hyperventilate and everything became a blur. I didn't recognize anything and began to panic. As I'm driving, I'm telling Denise in spasmodic breaths, "I don't know where I am. I can't believe it, I'm lost."

"What's wrong?" Denise kept asking. "What's wrong? Frankie, please pull the car over."

Stopping the car on the side of this narrow snow bound road, I forced the words out. "Denise, take the wheel. Take me back to the chalet."

As it turned out, we were only ¼ mile from the chalet. I was shaken up and couldn't for the life of me, imagine what was wrong with me. I thought I lost my mind. Back at the chalet, the only thing that kept going through my head was the images of the conference table in DA's private conference room. It had been filled with guns seized from drug dealers as a result of my undercover buys.

Days before this eventful weekend, the DA held a press conference, boasting about all of the weapons seized from drug dealers over the past few months. As the press core filtered into the conference room, the conference table, about 30 feet long, was massed with all the weapons seized. There must have been three hundred guns and rifles spread out on the table.

I was pacing back and forth in the chalet and still breathing heavily and struggling for air. Denise was frantic. "Frankie," she moaned, "You need to go to the hospital."

I didn't answer her. All I could think about was the damage these weapons can do to the human body. I was sweating, the perspiration dripping from my forehead. I didn't understand why I was feeling this way. Deep down inside, I feared for the detectives who might get hurt arresting these degenerates after I completed the narcotics buy. The thought of a cop getting killed during these arrests was sending me over the edge. I realized that I was in trouble and needed to talk to someone and soon. The only person I felt comfortable confiding in was a friend of mine, who happened to be a Catholic priest.

We left for New York immediately. As soon as I got home, I called him. Father John told me to come see him straightaway. He said that he would meet me in the rectory as soon as I got there. After talking with him about my feelings, what he told me was difficult to digest. He said that I was experiencing a nervous breakdown and needed to get away from my work for a few days. I needed to unwind from all the stress I was experiencing. "No calls or contact with anyone in your office." This floored me, I had no idea that my job could affect me this way. Apparently, I'm not as strong emotionally as I thought I was.

It just so happened that a friend of mind had a condo in Deerfield Beach, Florida. I vaguely explained the situation to Bryan while having coffee in the Bronxville Diner. He threw the condo keys at me. "Frankie, stay as long as you need too." Denise and I got on a plane the very next day. We spent five fantastic days relaxing on the beach, picnicking with wine, cheese and fresh fruit. I was able to decompress and sort out my life. When I returned to work, my batteries were charged and I was ready for Hector Cruz. Oh and most importantly, Denise and I were still an item.

Chapter Nineteen

Of course, the fact that I'd built a stone wall around myself, deflecting most advice I'd been given since I was a kid, pretty much said it all. Now it was time that I faced the music. The chief's Administrative Assistant, Liz, a young and attractive woman in her mid-thirties, had been trying to reach me all morning. When we finally connected, she said, "Where have you been? The Chief wants to see you immediately."

"Liz, I'd shut off my cell phone so I could get some sleep."

I had a feeling why the chief wanted to see me. I had to prepare for the ass reaming that I knew was coming. Shawn Daniels wasn't a street cop. He never worked the mean streets and couldn't know how to survive on them. Working with wise guys and drug dealers, my life could end if I twitched the wrong way. Daniels always worked inside the station house; he was clueless about running a successful street operation. Yet, he took all the credit for them when they went well but blamed the supervisor in charge if things went wrong. I didn't have to be a psychic to know that he was upset that I didn't call for back-up on the Cruz meeting. Believe me, he wasn't thinking about my safety. He was only interested in covering his ass with the DA if something went wrong.

Waiting to see the Chief felt like a kid in grade school who'd misbehaved in class and sent to the principal's office. He was hot tempered and could go from zero to sixty over nothing. I tried like hell to stay on his good side, but we were like oil and water.

Liz finally buzzed me into his office. He sat behind his desk, his face had a purple hue to it and I knew that I was about to be filleted. He was his typical self, disheveled and looking like an unmade bed. His tie, loosened at the collar, rested over his belt that surrounded his bulging midsection. He shouted for me to sit down and said, "Santorsola, the Cruz thing! The next time you pull a stunt like that, not requesting backup, you'll be back in uniform, shaking doors! Do I make myself clear!"

"Yes Chief, but...."

"Don't but me! You had plenty of time to call for backup. End of story!"

If I wanted to continue working with Baraka, I had no choice but to keep my trap shut. When the Chief saw that I wasn't gonna argue with him, he calmed down. That's when I thought I'd ease my way into telling him that Cruz was a big fish and I think if we let the first kilo buy go, I could work my way up the food chain. "Maybe," I said, Hector can take me to someone higher in the cartel."

Of course, the Chief didn't want to hear of it. Daniels had never been a narc and his lack of narcotic experience was hindering his investigative savvy. "Frank," he barked, "I'm not going to let thousands of dollars walk to see if Cruz will introduce you someone higher in his organization. We're playing it my way. Set it up with Cruz. If Cruz shows up with the coke, we're gonna lock him up. Is that understood? Believe me, if we lock him up, he'll give somebody up. Twenty-five years in the slam is a long time."

Daniels was covering his ass again. If something goes wrong with the buy/bust like, God forbid the money gets ripped off, he'd have hell to pay with the DA. He could be out of a job. His only concern was about the immediate success of the operation and never about having the balls to reach for the stars.

Chapter Twenty

It took a few days to set up the multi-kilo buy with Cruz. Of course, I wanted to buy as many kilos of coke that Cruz would sell. But Hector was cautious. "Popi, we'll do one or two at a time, until we get to know each other. Then the sky's the limit."

Cruz and I agreed on a price of $14,000 per kilo. Hector liked the idea of making the exchange in a hotel room. He said that it would provide us with more security. What he didn't know was that's the way I wanted the deal to go down. By taking care of business in the hotel, it would give me total control of the entire operation. By commanding the action, there's less chance of someone getting killed. The enforcement team's safety weighed heavily on my mind. Hector's men would be armed, that's a given. If cornered, they'd shoot it out rather than spend the rest of their lives in prison.

Matthews had booked several rooms on the third floor at the Ramada Inn in New Rochelle, N.Y. I'd set up the buy/bust in one of the rooms and the adjoining room will be used as the command center to monitor and record the operation. The irony of the whole thing is that the FBI field office was located on the ninth floor of this very hotel.

I had hours to kill before meeting Cruz. In order to prepare myself mentally, I picked up Baraka for an early dinner at Goomba Johnny's. There I could set the stage for tonight's meeting. I was now Frank Miranda, a half-ass wise guy and not an undercover cop. Hector had to believe who I said I was and more importantly, I had to believe it myself.

Hector was expected at the hotel at 9 p.m. Baraka and I got to the hotel two hours earlier so I could stay on top of things. Mike would play a limited role tonight, but Hector would expect him to be there. He'd be suspicious if he didn't show and that could jeopardize the deal.

As soon as we walked into the hotel, I was focused on our manpower controlling the place and its parking lot. Cruz wouldn't come alone; he would have armed men with him. Everybody's safety depended on limiting Hector's ability to overwhelm the operation using deadly force. In addition to this multi-layered action, the key to any successful field operation is the ability to communicate. It was crucial that the enforcement team be able to talk to one another, especially the men in the command center.

Everything was in place by 8:00 pm. Baraka was seated in the lobby and had no clue that Cruz was going to be locked up tonight. He was under the impression that Hector was going to walk out of the hotel with 28 grand in his pocket. It was better to keep him in the dark. His nerves might get the best of him and he might blow the whole thing.

I left him in the lobby and took the elevator to the third floor to room 303, to put the final touches on my props and to make sure that the command center and the guys in the enforcement team could hear me on the transmitter hidden inside of my wristwatch. The only thing I was focusing on now is locking Cruz up. I wasn't nervous, I was cool as cucumber. I can't explain it, I just was. I took the elevator back down to the lobby waiting for Hector to show up.

Right on time, Hector and another dirt-bag walked into the hotel. I thought, what a moron. If Hector had half a brain, he'd dress like a Wall Street stockbroker, not someone attending an MMA fight. Hector's buddy wasn't dressed any better. He was Spanish, short and stocky with a pencil thin mustache. I studied Hector's body language as he studied mine. I'm sure he was looking for anything out of the ordinary that said cop. Mike and Cruz's sidekick stayed in the lobby while Hector and I will make the exchange in my room.

Of course, Hector wanted to first see the money. But I had to go by the numbers for safety reasons. So, before I brought him upstairs, I wanted to make sure he wasn't armed. He reluctantly agreed to go into the lobby's bathroom so I could check him out for weapons. I didn't want him in the room with a gun and I sure as hell didn't want to be shot or held in a hostage situation.

It seemed like I was in a cone of silence as we entered the bathroom, it seemed surreal. Hector was talking, but all that I could see was his lips moving. My blood pressure was definitely elevated, but I couldn't let it show. My kids suddenly flashed through my mind; I couldn't imagine them living without their daddy. This was my reality. If things go bad, I could end up in the morgue.

In an instant, I was back in the real world. Hector decided to take the initiative and pat me down first. He touched me up and down, especially around my ankles, groin and waist. I was praying that he doesn't take a good look at my wristwatch and find the transmitter. He didn't give it a second glance. I'm sure he was anxious and wanted to get the sideshow on the road.

It was my turn to toss him. I began at his ankles, moving my hands up his pant legs to his groin, thoroughly feeling around his balls. I slid my hands around his waist and moved to his pants pockets. I felt something hard in his right front pocket. Huh, what do we have here, I thought? I quickly stuck my hand into his pocket and pulled out a 25-caliber automatic pistol. Probably the same one he'd shoved against my forehead a few days back. The thought of the slick son of a bitch ripping me off and killing me, coursed through my mind. No wonder I can't sleep at night. Believe me, all my senses were on overdrive. I really wanted this night to be over in the worst fuckin' way.

"The gun in my hand", I bellowed, "What is this? You planning to hurt me Hector?"

"No Popi, I thought I'd left it in the car. Lo siento."

Looking him dead in the eye, I removed the clip and racked the chamber back, ejecting the round in the chamber into my hand. Then placing the clip and the round in my pocket, I handed him back the gun. "Lo siento," I spat out, "I'm sorry too." It's the shit like this that stays with you. If I wasn't on top of my game that night, it could have ended my life.

Entering the elevator, I punched the keypad for the third floor. On the ride up I could barely look at him, I knew the kind of animal he was. He'd have no compulsion in shooting me, grabbing the $28,000 and leaving the hotel room without looking back. Once in the room, I called for the money to be brought from the command center so Hector could have a look-see. Cruz wasn't taking any chances; he began to search the entire room, looking in the closet, lifting up the mattress and checking the dresser for eavesdropping devices. The fuck failed to check the lamp on the desk, where the bug and camera was installed. After he finished his ritual and hadn't found anything, he looked relieved and began to relax. All the while, I sat in a corner chair, thinking about the world I lived in, it was dog-eat-dog. Life meant absolutely nothing to Hector. The only thing on his mind was money. Money was his God.

There was a knock on the door. Cracking open the door just enough to have a briefcase slid into the room, I picked it up and handed it to Hector. As he counted the money, my mind began to stray. I realized the kind of person I've become. In order to survive in this life, I had to become as hard a piece of steel. Now I understand why it's hard for me to let people in, emotionally. And I understand why it's hard to maintain a relationship with a woman. What woman could put up with me? My moodiness, the personality change when I drank and the stress of it all.

The coke was in Hector's car. Once Hector brought the cocaine up to the room, he was toast. Once we left the room, to protect the $28,0000, Joe Nulligan removed it from the briefcase, replaced it with it with play money and secured it in the command center. Down in the lobby, Mike looked pensive. He had no idea what was going on. We watched Hector and his goon walk out of the back door of the hotel and into the rear parking lot. It gave me time to talk to the command center. They knew exactly what was going down and on top of things. Detective Sidney posted in the lobby gave me a thumbs up as I walked by him.

Hector and his associate re-entered the hotel's lobby. Hector was carrying a brown gym bag. This was crunch time. Hector and I did our thing in the bathroom, while Mike and Cruz's associate remained in the lobby.

Back in the room, Hector handed me the gym bag. There were two bricks, kilo size, in the bag. I removed one of the bricks and placed it on the small corner table where I tested one of them. Bingo! I was buying Colombian cocaine made somewhere in the jungles of Colombia. I was disappointed that I wasn't allowed to work my way up into Hector's organization, but Hector was mine now and I was going to savor the moment.

Hector eyed the briefcase on the bed and wanted to leave the room. But I was stalling and held up the bottle of champagne. "Let's have a toast Hector!"

"Open it Popi! Our business here is done."

I smiled at Hector before giving the prearranged signal to call in the infantry. "Hector we're gonna do a lot of business together." In that moment, I felt a sense of triumph. I'd accomplished my mission. The feeling helped to relieved some of the pressure from a very demanding case. I'd accumulated a few more feathers in my cap. My record would reflect it when it came time for a promotion.

But, here's where it got sticky. What I didn't know was that Hector had smuggled a straight razor into the room that he'd hidden in small pocket on the underside of the gym bag. He somehow managed to remove it from the gym bag and slide it under his shirt sleeve without me seeing his treachery. When Cruz heard the door from the adjoining room come crashing down, he pulled out the razor from under his sleeve and lunged at me, trying to slice my jugular vein. Fortunately, before he could get to me, one of the onrushing detectives hit him on the side of his head with a blackjack and knocked him unconscious. As Hector regained consciousness and was helped to his feet, he looked over at me and said, "We're both dead."

I gave my lucky brown suit a rub and took the elevator down to the lobby to meet up with Mike. The look on his face said it all. He was shocked to see Hector and his sidekick handcuffed and dragged out of the hotel. As I drove Mike home, I tried to explain to him that I wasn't on board with arresting Hector, it was my superiors who made that decision. They unwisely believed that he would flip. Both of us knew that Hector would never flip. He knew the consequences for him and his family if he did.

Chapter Twenty-one

Assistant DA Falcone was adamant that the US Attorney's Office present Mike's work to the judge. He feared that the cartel would exercise revenge against Mike. He was right, Mike's life was in jeopardy and so was mine. By now, Cruz knew that Mike set him up with a cop and we'd have to be extra careful. I had similar worries, but deep down inside I wanted Mike to continue to work. Look, narcotics investigations are inherently dangerous, but as far as I was concerned, they fed into my need for excitement and that was the name of the game.

Falcone tried to convince Mike to rely on the results of the Cruz case to reduce his ten-year sentence. When Mike heard this, he went ballistic and would have none of it. He hollered that he was innocent of drug trafficking and wanted to continue to work until he could prove it. He insisted that his look alike cousin Ayman was guilty of the charges and not him. He maintained that the police and the DEA picked him up instead of his cousin, in the final stages of the investigation. He cried that they didn't take the time to distinguish between him and his cousin, who has the same first name as he does. To them, he said, he was just another Arab. Since Mike's arrest, his cousin fled to the middle east and is in hiding.

 Falcone asked me to talk Mike into presenting his work to the court, but like I said, I didn't see it that way. Not as long as Baraka could keep me busy by reeling in more big fish like Cruz. Anyway, it wasn't up to me. It was up to Mike and his attorney.

Regarding Cruz, he spent a few weeks in jail. Hector was bailed out by a Colombian Real Estate magnate from Washington Heights, who posted $250,000. You don't have to be a genius to figure it out. Hector's benefactor had to be connected to the Medellin Drug Cartel. Cruz disappeared the very next day. Losing $250,000 was a drop in the bucked for the cartel, they were making billions.

Chapter Twenty-two

I couldn't help it; I loved the eagerness of the hunt. Being an undercover cop became more than a job for me, it was my own personal addiction that I couldn't get enough of. It wasn't long before Baraka had another case lined up and I couldn't wait for the action to start. A friend of his knew of Mike's predicament and was willing to introduce him to an Israeli national, who he'd met in a New York City nightclub. After some chit-chat, he found out that the guy was in the heroin trade. Leo confided to Mike that the fellow wanted to get rid of a couple of kilograms of heroin that he had stashed in his girlfriend's apartment. She was scared and wanted them out of the house. Of course, Mike was excited and wanted to meet him. Leo arranged a meeting with Mordechay Zisser, the Jewish drug dealer, in Sofia's, Italian restaurant in South Yonkers.

After meeting Zisser, Mike said that he was in his sixties and looked like he just came off of Miami Beach. Tall, dark and good looking and had a full head of pure white hair that he wore in a ponytail. The only thing missing were the gold earrings. When Mike told me that the guy wanted $125,000 per kilo, alarms went off right away. The street price, depending on purity, should wholesale for about $250,000 per kilo. "Mike, the price is too low," there has to be something wrong with the deal." My instincts told me so, and I trusted my gut. Then there was Zisser, a Jewish drug dealer, hum? Not that anyone is immune to the business of dealing drugs, but this was a first. If there was a Jewish drug ring around, I hadn't heard about it. My antennas were up about this guy and who he was connected to.

There's that word trust again. I trust my instincts. Between my lucky brown suit and my instincts, they've never failed me. Trust has only five letters, but what a word. It's friendship, honor, respect, faith, dependency and maybe other words I can't think of right now. It's the way I want to conduct my life, but as for a lot of us, we get distracted by life's bumps in the road and then something happens that brings us back to what we believe in. Do I take a chance and trust that Mike won't try to burn me? Maybe it's the rebellious side of me always wanting to push the envelope. I decided to roll the dice and take a chance on him. Baraka had set up a meeting on Friday night with

Mordechay at Fellini's Restaurant on Columbus Avenue in Manhattan, between 77th and 78th Street.

Mordechay was already seated by the picture window of the traditionally decorated Italian restaurant when Mike and I walked in. He was impeccably dressed, wearing an expensive black pinstriped suit, a red tie with an expensive gold tie pin and matching cuff links. The Rolex with a diamond bezel completed the ensemble. He stood as we walked over to the table and shook hands. As soon as we sat, I noticed flashes of light coming from the street. It was springtime and raining, so I'm thinking that the flashes of light was lightning. They continued through most of our dinner as we discussed the price for the heroin and where the exchange would take place.

I continued to press Mordechay on why the price was so low. In his suave and debonair demeanor, said that the price is low only because he is getting out of the drug business and his girlfriend wants them out of the house. His explanation didn't make any sense to me. I'm thinking that he could have secured the heroin somewhere else and sold them at market value. Why lose a ton of money? I didn't let on that I didn't believe him and didn't trust him as far as I could throw him. I'd have to let his tale play itself out. I looked over at Mike who sat pensively next to me. From the look on his face, I didn't think that he bought Mordechay's act either. Before we finished dinner, Zisser removed a small tin foil packet from his suit jacket pocket, slipped it under his table napkin and pushed the napkin over to me. "Frank, test it later, it's 85% pure."

We exchanged cell numbers and agreed to meet in two hours at the Days Inn, up on West 94th Street. I threw $150.00 on the table and then Mike and I walked outside into the pouring rain. In case the deal went through, I had the money placed into a black leather shoulder bag and secured in the evidence room. As Mike and I headed for the hotel, I pulled over on Columbus Avenue and called the duty officer, briefing him on the nights events and that I was meeting Mordechay in two hours at the Day's Inn on west 94th Street. Detective Serrano said he'd notify the enforcement team and they'd have everything ready for me at the hotel. Now it was a game of show and tell. I felt that adrenaline rush again as we drove north to the hotel. I was so excited, the only thing I was thinking about was how the night was going to play out. I was so wrapped up in having everything and everyone in place at the hotel that I didn't notice the group of cars following behind me. In all honesty, I probably wouldn't have seen them anyway, it was raining cats and dogs and all I could see were the headlights behind me.

Mike and I got to the hotel before the enforcement team and the guys who'd monitor the case from the adjoining room. It would be business as usual. We'd do it by the numbers just like we did in the Cruz case. A little after 1:00 a.m. Deputy Chief Achim walked into the hotel lobby carrying a large black leather bag. I followed him into the lobby's bathroom and he handed me the transmitter watch and the key card to room 501.

Mike stood there like he was watching a one act play unfold. "Frank,"the Deputy Chief said, "the place is saturated with our men. Let's make sure we have good audio." He then took the elevator up to room 503.

Damn right I'm gonna make sure that the audio is working, my ass is on the line. Baraka once again took a seat in the lobby as I took the elevator up to the room 501. In the room I tested the powdery material that Mordechay slipped to me at dinner. It tested positive for heroin. At the same time my cell phone rang. It was Mordechay and he wanted to know if I was set with the money. "Of course, I'm all set. Are you ready on your end?"

"Yes, my friend. I have them wrapped like Hanukkah gifts for you."

This is where things started to go south. The slippery bastard then said, "Instead of us doing business in the hotel, let's make the exchange in the parking lot of the hotel at Kennedy Airport."

My suspicions about him were on target. There was definitely something rotten going on and I knew it. "Mordechay," I yelled, "I'm not gonna anywhere with the fuckin' money! Got it!"

"I just thought it would be easier to do at the airport, less people around."
I exploded. "What the fuck are you talking about? Less people around? It's just me and you in a hotel room. We deal here or I walk."

"Okay, Okay. Don't get excited. I'm down the street. I'll be there in ten minutes."

Mike and I were waiting for him when he waltzed into the lobby at about 1:30 a.m. Mike took a seat on one of the couches in the lobby and I repeated the Cruz thing in the men's room with Mordechay. There was no way that I was gonna let him get a gun upstairs. But unlike Hector, he was clean. I never took my eyes off of him until we got to the room.

As soon as we walked into the room, Zisser said hastily, "I want to see the money."

"Where's the dope, I snapped!"

We weren't in the room for more than three minutes when all of a sudden, there were several loud thuds on my hotel room door. There was lots of radio traffic coming from the hallway. I stepped back away from the door, confused, stunned, glaring over at Mordechay who had a twenty-mission stare etched on his face.

I heard voices in the hallway screaming, "Don't hit the door! The guy's a cop!" I was dazed and didn't know what to think. From the adjoining room, Achim ran into my room, in a panic. "Frankie, DEA almost took the door down. They're all over the place. This guy Mordechay is a DEA informant. They thought you were a legitimate target. They were gonna lock you up and seize the money."

Son of a bitch! This could have ended up a tragedy tonight if DEA agents weren't confronted in the hotel garage. Agents and detectives could have been killed in a shootout. The DEA apparently didn't do their due diligence.

94

I was supposed to be a mob connected guy. If they thoroughly examined who I said I was and found that Frank Miranda might not be who he said he is, they may have taken a prudent approach to tonight's action. Apparently, they were only interested in locking me up and seizing the money. In the end, my instincts were right. The deal with Zisser smelled from beginning to end.

Chapter Twenty-three

I'd taken a few days off to relax from the DEA fiasco from the other night. Besides, the powers that be didn't want me to come back to work unless I had a clear head. That wasn't the case for Baraka, he didn't stop pursuing targets. Staying out of prison is a great motivator. The other night Mike was hanging out at Petra's, an Arabic Nightclub on 10th Avenue and West 34th Street in Manhattan. He knew through one of his brother-in-laws that movers and shakers in the drug business frequented the place. His brother-in-law Salam had befriended the club's owner, Yousef Nebor, an Egyptian National. Yousef also dabbled in the heroin trade, so Mike figured that Petra's was a good a place to connect with another drug dealer.

One night while sitting at the bar, Mike met a guy named Louie DeFalco. While chatting, DeFalco said that he owned a string of laundromats in the West Bronx. During their conversation, Mike said that he had fell on hard times and is now making ends meet by peddling drugs. DeFalco took to Mike immediately. Like I said, Mike naturally had the ability to get people to like him. Louie confided that he knew connected people and how to get his hands-on high-grade heroin. Baraka, a cunning individual, planted the seed in Louie's head that he had a friend who was always looking for product to supply his dopers in Atlantic City. DeFalco took the bait, hook line and sinker and wanted Mike to arrange a meeting with his friend. A meeting was set up for the following evening at the night club.

Before the meeting, I had Intel run a background on DeFalco. It turned out that DeFalco had an arrest sheet as long as my arm. By age forty-five he had five felony convictions under his belt. He was arrested for assault with a deadly weapon but beat the rap because the victim refused to press charges. Louie, now forty-seven, is short, muscular, with jet black hair, dark brown eyes and dresses to the nines. It seems that Mike and I are gelling as a team. I lowered my guard, breaking the primary rule of not getting close to an informant, but the cases we were making was feeding my ego and keeping my need for excitement in full gear.

Arabic music was blaring from the dance floor as we walked into the nightclub. Mike nudged me as he noticed DeFalco standing at the far end of the bar. Louie spotted us and waved us over. His dark piercing eyes burned through me as Mike introduced me. From the get-go, he was seizing me up. But like I said, I did my homework and knew all about him. Maybe because of my dyslexia, I'm able to focus more, so nothing escapes me, especially when my ass is on the line. We settled on what we were drinking. DeFalco got the bartender's attention. "My friend Frank will have a Dewar's, with a little ice, a Heineken for Mike and give me another Tanqueray and tonic.

The bouzouki band was playing as Arabic belly dancers performed. Some patrons danced with other men and some danced alone, as they tossed money at the performers. The music was so loud that it was difficult to have a conversation. The thought crossed my mind that Louie and Yousef Nebor were probably in the heroin business together. My gut is usually right on the money.

DeFalco spotted a table emptying off the dance floor and said, "Let's grab it before someone else takes it." We brought our drinks with us, sat and got a bird's eye view of the belly dancers gyrating to the melodic Arabic music. It wasn't long before Yousef Nebor made his way over from the kitchen area. Yousef was pencil thin, over six-feet tall, dressed all in black and his dark hair was slicked back exposing his receding hair line. He signaled for the waiter. "A bottle of our best champagne. I see that you're new to my club. Gentlemen, I'm sending over some food to go with the champagne. Enjoy the girls and the music." This surprised me. Why would Yousef pay special attention to us? I sensed that Yousef and DeFalco knew each other. Maybe I was the proverbial lamb being led to slaughter. The waiter was back with the champagne and glasses, pouring us each a glass of the bubbly. The food came a little later. Louie wasted no time. "Mike tells me you're looking for some new product?"

"Mike's right. Of course, depending on the purity and price."

Feeling the burn from his piercing eyes, DeFalco, all business said, "Frank, I have what you're looking for. Feel like taking a ride?"

Again, my instincts told me that something was wrong, but I couldn't say no. By the look on Mike's face, he was uneasy too.

"Where to?" I asked.

Louie with a half-ass grin replied, "Brooklyn, just over the Brooklyn Bridge."

We finished the rolled grape leaves filled with rice and washed them down with the rest of the Dom Perignon. "I'm parked in front," DeFalco said with a smile. "Follow me, I'm driving a white Mercedes Benz." We were out the door in short order. I was feeling uneasy as Mike and I got into the Lincoln. Something wasn't right and I realized that I wasn't in control of the situation we were in. We made a U-turn and followed DeFalco out of Manhattan, over the Brooklyn Bridge and into Brooklyn.

DeFalco took us east on Atlantic Avenue to Nevins Street, heading south and then turned onto Union Street, where we followed him into the Parkside Service Center. We parked diagonally from him. This is where the evening went up-side down. I had that bad feeling in the pit of my stomach. Louie had no intention of selling me heroin, tonight or ever. It was a total set up to draw me out to find out if I was a cop. If I wasn't so bullheaded, Mike and I wouldn't be in this situation. I guess my ego wouldn't let me forget my childhood. They all thought I would never amount to anything, even my parents. I had to prove to everyone that I was the best at undercover work, including myself.

DeFalco got out of his car, popped the trunk of the Benz and waved us over. If Mike knew what was racing through my head, he would have never gotten out of the car. I grabbed my pistol from under the front seat as Mike and I headed for the Benz. Standing over the trunk, there were two kilo size bricks, wrapped in brown paper, sitting inside. DeFalco waited to see what I was gonna do. I'm sure he thought that I would arrest him on the spot if I were a cop and in return, I'd probably only find a harmless substance in the packages instead of heroin. "Louie," I growled, "I didn't come prepared to test your dope."

From the corner of my eye, I saw two men sitting in a black Chevrolet parked just a few cars away. I decided that it was time for Mike and I to make an Irish exit. Louie and his goons were running the show and not me. I got us into a dangerous situation that I needed to quickly get out of it.

"Louie," I said, "we'll pick this up another time. I'm getting a bad feeling about the whole thing. Let's go Mike!"

Mike and I beat feet for the Lincoln. The two guys in the Chevy jumped out of the car and started for us. I saw by the menacing look on their faces, that they were out for blood and planned to find out who I was. We picked up our pace across the parking lot and quickly got into the car. I pulled my gun from under my sports jacket and threw it on my lap, put the car in drive and sped out of the lot. I wasn't looking back. I'm pretty sure, at the very least, I would have received a beating if they got their hands on me, if I didn't cry cop. Defalco would have apologized, said he had to make sure I wasn't a cop and would have ultimately done business with me. I wasn't gonna take any chances and wait around to see what was going to happen, I was getting the hell out of there.

Chapter Twenty-four

I remember the first real date I had with Denise. I threw on a navy-blue sports jacket, a white button-down dress shirt, silk tie, a pair of jeans, brown Monk shoes and scrambled out the door. I looked as good as I knew how. Denise's building overlooked the Henry Hudson Parkway in the Bronx. She was standing in front of her ten-story apartment building, when I rolled up. She looked gorgeous standing there in a bronze silky cocktail dress, held up by spaghetti straps and matching bronze pumps with little bows. She literally took my breath away, but somehow I managed to mumble, "Hey Denise, you look beautiful. I've made an 8:30 p.m. reservation at "iL Vagabondo restaurant" on East 62nd Street in Manhattan." It's a casual restaurant with an Italian cuisine. It even had a bocce court in the basement. Bocce is an Italian game that some think resembles bowling. It has finer points, like shuffleboard, some say. The beauty of it is you can play a game or two of bocce before or after you dine.

The Maître d' walked us over to our table near the stairwell that lead down to the bocce court. The table was dressed in a red and white checkered tablecloth, white linen napkins, water, wine glasses and silverware. A white rose was in a vase in the center of the table. Before we ordered, Denise asked to see the bocce court. Hand in hand, we took the stairs down to the court. There was a group of people gathered around one of the two courts, playing, having fun socializing, while drinking wine and beer.

"Frankie, I've never played bocce."

"I played it as a kid. It was my grandfather's favorite game."

We watched for ten minutes as I explained how the game was being played. The rules are not difficult and Denise got an understanding right away. Returning to our table, Denise was grinning from ear to ear. "Frankie, thanks for taking me to this fantastic restaurant. It's so nice getting to know you."

Get to know me? Well, if Denise gets to know me, I'm not sure if she'll stick around. There's so much drama in my life right now. It might frighten her away. I'm still battling my ex-wife over visitation rights with my daughters and then there's the constant struggle with dyslexia that affects my everyday life. For example, my thoughts are sometimes in reverse and it takes a few seconds to straighten them out, especially in conversation. I don't want to say anything to Denise that comes out the wrong way. Then there's the being raised in a traditional Italian family, where my dad was very strict. I guess you could say he was old school in many ways. The upside of his parenting was that he gave me and my brother the tools we needed to do the kind of work we do.

We both ordered the signature dish, Veal Parmesan, house salad and a bottle of Santa Margarita, a white wine. Their veal dish is prepared a little differently than most, the chef uses Munster cheese instead of Mozzarella. It really compliments the dish and it's seasoned with Italian breadcrumbs, grated parmigiana regiano cheese, oregano, dried basil and cayenne pepper. The food was delicious and the wine was superb. It was the first time in a long while that I truly felt comfortable with another woman. She seemed easy to get to know. Besides being gorgeous, she had an innocent way about her. I couldn't help but think that her life was much simpler than mine, even though she danced in a strip club and had to deal with sleazy men daily.

The night was magical. I saw it in her eyes that we were connected in a special way. When I dropped her off, I didn't want to be away from her. I knew that, that very night, I'd fallen in love with her. Before she got out of the car I leaned in, her eyes softly met mine and we kissed for what seemed like hours.

That night I told Denise that I was an undercover cop. She surprised me by what she said. "I knew that you weren't like most men, you were different. You never made me feel like you were sexually dissecting me. You weren't like the rest of the guys that stuffed money into my G-string. You never did."

By my very nature, I don't trust anyone at first glance. It takes a long time to figure out where they are coming from. Most people I meet have hidden agendas and usually want something from me. But with Denise it was different, I trusted her instinctively. From that night on, we've never been apart. I knew our souls were connected and someday we'd be together. We were soulmates and both of us knew it to be true.

Chapter Twenty-five

Baraka and I had been working together for a year and a half and making some of the biggest narcotics cases in the metropolitan area. There was no question about it, he was responsible for successful prosecutions involving some of the biggest drug dealers in the New York. I was sure that the US Attorney's Office would recommend that Mike be spared going to prison. That wasn't good enough for Mike, he wanted to keep working and that was fine with me. "Frank, I'm innocent. Not going to jail is not good enough. I need my conviction to be overturned."

"Mike, believe me, the US Attorney's Office doesn't want the conviction overturned, they won't admit that they screwed up. Getting your cousin to return from the Middle East and confess is a pipe dream. Why would he come back? Why would he face going to federal prison?"

"My mother has been in touch with her sister in Jordan and she's been putting pressure on her. She's hoping that her sister is going to force her son to come back to the states to face the music."

I knew that the AUSA John Kenny, in the US Attorney's Office, would not be interested in overturning Mike's conviction. They had nothing to gain. They'd have to admit in court that they convicted the wrong guy. I knew that I'd have to get the ball rolling and test the waters to see how things would shake out. I owed Mike that much.

The very next day, Mike called me and said that his cousin called, telling him that he was willing to return to the states and confess that he was the one who should have been prosecuted.

Now that was startling news! I immediately took the stairwell up to Robert Falcone's office. He seemed less than his cool, levelheaded self when I walked into his office. He had the word stress written all over his face. In any event, I was about to throw him a curve ball that would give him the worst case of acid reflux he ever had. I filled him in on Ayman Hanni returning to the states to clear his cousin Mike. But Robert wouldn't hear any of it. Basically, he said if I was willing to ruin my career on Baraka's contrived tale that it was fine with him, but he wasn't going to. Falcone was thinking that I was just some over worked cop who'd been in the trenches too long. "Frank, I have a lot of work to do. Now if I were you, I'd let it go."

"You know what, Robert? In my line of work, my life is on the line. All that needs to happen is the wrong word said, my body language is wrong, more sweat than a situation warrants and I'm history. I've lived with wise guys for years. I knew when I was in the presence of these guys when arrest warrants were executed and I never once folded. And you're telling me I'm taking a risk with my career by doing the right thing here? Robert, it's a fuckin' cakewalk compared to what I do every day to earn a living. So, who's kidding who? My career, what career? Pal, I don't know what you're gonna do about Baraka's cousin, but I'm not gonna worry about my fucking career."

I slammed the door as I stormed out of his office. But with resolve, I vowed to blow through the very people who are supposed to make the criminal justice system work. I'd find a way to take Mike's cousin's confession when he returned.

Chapter Twenty-six

All I could think about was the violence that me and other cops are exposed too. I guess we condition ourselves to get used to it and keep everything inside of us, for as long as we can. But, at some point something has to give. Over time, the violence that man can inflict on his fellow man, eats away at you, both mentally and physically. Some of us, as I've said, take to the bottle; some to drugs and others to violence, even to the point of taking their own lives. One thing is for sure, at least it is for me, you need someone in your life who loves and understands you; to hold things together, so you can come to grips with your life. Without that, most cops end up divorced, with broken relationships with their kids and their extended families.

I've really tried to maintain a relationship with my daughters. But, unfortunately, it hasn't worked out. I think, because of my innate nature and the life I live, my relationship with my girls was destined to fail. Little by little, I became tough as nails, with little compassion and understanding for most people and I guess my daughters saw that. I fooled myself into thinking that I could separate the worlds I lived in, the undercover cop and the father of two precious little girls. But I couldn't. I thought I could keep Frank Santorsola separate from the world I lived in, but it didn't work out that way. My two worlds collided and I drove away the people closest to me.

It hit me extremely hard when two young girls were murdered recently by some maniac. It was difficult for me not to think of my girls and not being there to protect them. The murdered girls were of Hispanic descent. They were killed and then dumped on the roadside in Harrison, NY by an ex-Cuban military officer, who fled from Cuba with money he embezzled from the Castro government.

Through a confidential informant, Nulligan and I found out that the killer was renting a basement apartment on Gun Hill Road in the Bronx. The building was under demolition at the time. We pressured the buildings super to give us a pass key to Perez's apartment and waited for the slug to return home. It was the month of July, the apartment was hot with no fans or air-conditioning. As we waited, the building was being demolished above us. Cockroaches were raining down on us as the wrecking ball continued to slam into the building. Finally, after almost two days without sleep, sometime around 10:00 a.m., we heard the key turn in the door lock. Joe and I stood on each side of the door. When Perez walked in, we lunged at him, pressing our pistols on each side of his head. I'm dizzy from lack of sleep, forcing his body up against the wall, then jerking his arms behind his back and handcuffing him. I can't tell you how satisfied I felt to have collared the guy.

It just so happened that the day that Joe and I arrested Perez, I had scheduled visitation and was going to pick up my two daughters. Although I hadn't slept in two days, there was no way that I wasn't going to see my girls. They were my life and kept me grounded in this topsy-turvy world I live in. In retrospect, picking them up wasn't the smartest thing I've ever done. My body ached from lack of sleep and I couldn't keep my eyes open, much less drive a car. My ex-wife had gotten re-married and she and her husband had bought a house in Mt. Kisco, NY. It was about an hour north from where I was living at the time. The girls had just gotten home from school when I pulled up in front of their house. I gotta say, when I saw them standing there, I saw how vulnerable and innocent they were. They were waiting for their daddy. I realized that they were the causalities of my failures. My heart sunk, it was completely crushed. I came to the realization that my heart had hardened, even towards my own family. I was incapable of compassion. For this, I'm asking for prayers and understanding.

As soon as they got into the car, I told my oldest daughter Francesca, who was sixteen, at the time, that I was extremely tired and to make sure that I stayed awake on our drive to Bronxville. I remember her nudging my face with her hands several times when she saw my eyes begin to close. "Thanks sweetie. Don't let daddy fall asleep." God must have been with us because we made it to my apartment alive. As soon as we entered the apartment, I told Denise that I was fried, headed for the bedroom and passed out on my bed. Denise took good care of them, cooking them dinner and making excuses of why their daddy was asleep. She had them home by eight o'clock, as instructed by the court order. I must have slept through the night and half the next day. Having a lasting relationship with me is a lot for anyone to handle. The job has a way of coming between you and your loved ones.

Chapter Twenty-seven

My court ordered visitation was on every Tuesday and Thursday night. I mentioned that my daughters were living with their mother Helen and step-father, in Mt. Kisco, NY at the time. If work permitted, I'd drive up to Mt. Kisco and we'd usually have dinner at my mom's house, or I'd take them to a local restaurant in the immediate area. Believe me, I saw them regularly for years until they went to college. Everything changed after that.

The last time I remember seeing them is when I picked them up in Mt. Kisco after work. We decided to have dinner at Friendly's restaurant on Main Street, which was only a short distance from their house. I guess we arrived at the restaurant about 7:00 p.m. We sat in a booth near the front door. The waitress came over and took our drink order as we chatted about how they were doing with their school grades and how they were getting along with their new stepfather. The waitress came over with our sodas and I think we all ordered burgers and french fries. Before she returned with the food, my youngest daughter, Katie, out of the blue asked, "Daddy, is it true that you're just like the mafia guys you put in jail?" I was taken back by her question. For a minute I looked at Katie and was a loss for words. Francesca sat there staring at me and waiting for my reply. The waitress returned with our food and set it down in front of us.

After getting my thoughts together, I asked Katie, "Katie, why would you ask me that?"

"Well, are you?"

"No, sweetheart, I'm not. I'm a policeman who keeps you and your mommy safe from the people like that. People might hurt mommy and your sister."

That took the wind out of my sails. I hardly ate, just staring at my plate. Not much was said after that. Sadly, it was the last time I saw my daughters after I dropped them off at home. They refused to see me after that night. Although I've tried many times to reconcile with them, they want nothing to do with me. I understand that they're both married and living somewhere in Connecticut. I cried my last tear some years ago when a friend of mine had to sit me down after karate class. He told me that over the weekend, he attended my daughter Francesca's wedding. I cried like a baby for hours after he told me. My heart was broken. Today, I have no more tears to cry. It crushes me inside if I dwell on it. I pray to God that someday we can reconnect. Our relationship doesn't have to be a father, daughter relationship, but just something. I need to know that they are okay.

Now that I've vented, it's time to get back to the business at hand. Louis DeFalco was unfinished business. I've been sitting on his laundromat in the Bronx for about a week, but the cockroach hasn't shown up. As it turned out, there was a good reason for him not showing up at his place of business. His body had washed up, tangled in the rocks that surrounded the Statue of Liberty. The Medical Examiner's Office reported that he died of two gun shots from a 9mm pistol to the back of his head. So they say, live by the sword, die by the sword. I figured that Louie must have stepped on the wrong toes and it got him killed.

Chapter Twenty-eight

Nothing in life is as simple as it seems. It turned out that Baraka's cousin was not as forthcoming as Mike's mother had hoped. In several conversations with Mike, I learned that his cousin got cold feet and was reluctant to come to the states to exonerate Mike. After pressure from his tribal community in Jordan, the tribal members had a talking with him and persuaded him to honor his commitment to clear his cousin.

Ayman Hanni hadn't contacted his cousin with his flight information, so no one knew exactly when he was coming into the country. It became a waiting game. I can't say that I slept much, thinking about what I was gonna do when I met with him. I'd be going against the proverbial establishment and probably kissing my career goodbye. At this point in my life, my career was everything. I lived for it, it was my personal identity, policing is who I am.

Mike finally called, telling me that his cousin was in town, but wouldn't let him know where he was staying. I told him to call me as soon as he hears back from his cousin to get the ball rolling. It was about a week later, Mike called me again. This time I could hear the excitement in his voice, his cousin was ready to give his statement. His cousin's confession would be unprecedented, especially in the federal system. I was sticking my neck out as far it would go. I told him that they should meet me the following morning at 7:45a.m. on the courthouse steps.

I laid awake all-night thinking, where was this gonna end? Would I be fired? Would I be placed in the rubber gun squad and left out to dry until I couldn't take it any longer and retire? I prepared myself to test the sharp edge of the criminal justice system. Yes, I was rolling the dice and hoping it didn't turn up snake eyes. What the hell, I've always taken chances in my life. That's how I was raised. My dad always said, "Frankie, if you're going to amount to anything in your in your life you can't play it safe. You'll need to take chances.

Right or wrong, that's how I like to play it. I knew that Mike was innocent, come hell or high water, I was taking his cousin's confession.

Mike and his cousin were waiting in front of the building, just as planned. They looked like identical twins. I actually did a double take, unable to distinguish them apart for a minute. They even dressed the same; white dress shirt, black slacks, squared toed black shoes, and Louis Vuitton sunglasses.

I brought them up to the fourth floor and made them comfortable in the DA's office interrogation room. I took a chair at the table across from Ayman Hanni. A tape recorder was placed in front of Hanni and turned on. The rest is history. He began to construct the international narcotics case and all the people involved. Most importantly he exonerated his cousin Mike.

The easy part was over. But now came the hard part. I left the room for a minute, soon returning with a copy of the video and audio tapes and handed them to Mike. "Give them to your attorney."

As soon as Mike and his cousin left, I headed upstairs to Falcone's office. I walked in without knocking. He looked a bit surprised to see me this early in the day. Standing in front of his desk I said, "Robert, I don't want you to hear this from anyone else." He sat up in his chair. "Uh oh, I have a feeling I'm not going to like what you're going to say."

I didn't pull any punches, there were none to pull. "I just finished video and audio-taping Mike Baraka's cousin's confession. In a nutshell, he admitted that it was he and not Mike who distributed heroin for Mickey Calise. You prosecuted the wrong guy."

The color left his face. "You did what?"

"Just what I said, I gave Mike a copy of the tapes and told him to give them to his attorney. You gotta make choices Robert and I've made mine."

My office was boxed in and they had no option but to accept the fact that Mike was innocent and they convicted the wrong guy. If they could have fired me, they would have. But the press was all over the story and there was nothing they could do to me. I was hero in everybody's eyes, well maybe not to some of the prosecutors in my office.

A few weeks had passed and a court hearing was scheduled to rule on whether or not Mike's conviction would be vacated. Federal Judge Sposato granted Mike a writ of coram nobis, vacating the judgment of conviction on all counts. He was a free man.

As for Ayman Hanni, he was sentenced to the ten years that his cousin was supposed to do. He was paroled after serving only thirty-seven months in federal prison. Ya know, a leopard doesn't change his spots. Only six months out of prison and he was arrested again. A wealthy businessman hired him to murder an attorney after the two had a fist fight in a restaurant over cigarette smoke blown in his face by the attorney. The businessman cooked up the murder plot after the attorney charged him with assault and sued him for $3 million dollars. The businessman reached out to a buddy to help him find a hit man. The friend, who knew Hanni, got in touch with him. The friend got cold feet and contacted my office. We wired him and set up a meeting with the businessman and Hanni. The meeting took place in the study of the businessman's twenty-five room mansion, that was built on a hundred of the most beautiful acres in up-state New York. I listened to the conversation a few days later. He tells Hanni, "I want this guy dead! I can't do it myself because I would be the prime suspect in the attorney's murder as a result of the assault charge and the $3 million-dollar lawsuit." Hanni agreed to kill the attorney for ten thousand dollars. He wanted half up front and the other half when he reads about it in the newspaper. You can actually hear the businessman count out $5 grand and hand it to Hanni. "Get it done by next week."

Hanni and the businessman were arrested the following day by detectives from my office. They had no defense and plead guilty to the charge of conspiracy to commit murder.

Chapter Twenty-nine

When I moved out of the shit-hole apartment I rented in the Bronx and moved in with Denise, I began to live like a human being again. Like I said, the fallout from the divorce from Helen brought me to the lowest point in my life. The idea of family being the most important thing in my life somehow got away from me. I was alone for a few years, wallowing in my own self-imposed misery. My double life of an undercover cop, trying to keep my head screwed on straight, seemed an impossible task at the time. I didn't know where to turn, so I turned to alcohol to deaden the pain like other cops.

Joe Nulligan called me one day to tell me about an experience he had on a detail with another squad detective. He and the detective were assigned to meet with a Lieutenant form another command regarding a burglary ring plaguing the Westchester/Greenwich, Ct. area. Joe said that it was ten in the morning when he and the detective headed down to the parking garage to pick up their car for the drive to Greenwich PD. The detective, who will go unnamed, asked Joe to stop by his car before leaving. Joe pulled up to the detective's unmarked police car and the detective got out and retrieved a liter size plastic bottle.

As soon as he got back into Joe's car, Joe said that the detective unscrewed the bottle cap and began drinking. It turned out that he was drinking vodka. The detective turned to Joe asked if he wanted a taste. He said, "Joe, you know the drill, pop some gum in your mouth and nobody will know you've been drinking." By the time they reached the Greenwich PD the detective was sloshed out of his mind. Joe said that he had to help him into the PD. He staggered as they were escorted to the Lieutenant's office. Bleary-eyed and slurring his words, the Lieutenant couldn't help but notice that Joe's partner was drunk. He told Joe to get the guy out of his office; their meeting was over. Soon after, the Lieutenant called Deputy Chief Achim and told him that his detective was drunk and to never send him back to his PD again. All Joe knew is that when they got back to the office, the detective was brought to the Chief's office and as far as he knows no disciplinary action was taken. The guy was a safety risk to all of us. Obviously, no one in the squad wanted to work with the guy and as far as I knew he continued to drink until he retired.

Moving in with Denise MacKenzie changed all that around for me. We pooled our money and rented a one bedroom walk up on the fifth floor on Sagamore Road in Bronxville, New York. My divorce from Helen took a lot out of me. Before Denise it was easy for me to hide my sorrow in alcohol. The burn marks from the ordeal hurt the same today as they did a few years ago, but I no longer self-medicate. Now that Denise is in my life, I put all my energy into rebuilding my life. Her zest for life and upbeat attitude was an inspiration for me to get my life back on track. I finally realized that life's a gift and I didn't want it to slip away without embracing all of it.

As a couple, we didn't socialize much, mainly because I didn't like meeting new people. When we did get out, it was usually with other cops and their wives or girlfriends. It's funny, most cops feel more comfortable socializing with other cops. We don't have to pretend to be someone we're not. We can be ourselves, talk and laugh about the aspects of the job that most civilians might find offensive. Plus, you never know who the other guests might be related to. Staying under the radar is my first commandment. I can't tell you how many times I've been approached at a party by someone who found out that I was a cop and asked if I could fix a parking ticket. What a put down for a cop. What do they think, we're all corrupt?

Since I didn't own any furniture, Denise furnished the apartment with modern style furniture she brought from her rented apartment in the Bronx. After Baraka won his freedom, I was in limbo for a few weeks, hanging out at the apartment, listening to my best-loved music and cooking my favorite meals. After two weeks, I was energized and ready to sink my teeth into something new. I know me, I needed to stay busy and keep my juices flowing. Denise, on the other hand was happy to see me relax and stay home. She said that I needed the time off to unwind.

When I got back to work, it was rumored that I've been lined up with another case. I started to ask around the office to find out what it was about, but no one knew anything. If they did, they were keeping it to themselves. To set the stage for my new assignment, I have to begin with the homicide of Leonard Capolla. Leonard was the co-owner of C&C Carting, a private sanitation company, that was on Gun Hill Road in the Bronx. The initial police report indicated that Capolla had been shot twice in the back of the head with a small caliber pistol. Violent death is nothing new to me. Believe me, it's what nightmares are made of. On a superficial level, death hardens most police officers. Cops can become emotionless to the violence. It allows us to do our job, especially homicide detectives.

The first autopsy I attended was a real eye-opener. The doctor had the corpse of a young man in his thirties; he had been shot to death. He was laid open from his sternum to his crotch on Medical Examiner's table. The M.E. first removed the cadaver's heart, liver, lungs and stomach. The contents of the stomach were examined to see what the guy last digested. He then dissected the organs and weighted them for testing. Believe me, this is hard to stomach, pardon the pun, but somehow, I managed to get through it without throwing my guts up. What happened next blew my freakin' mind. He was about to saw the guy's skull cap off and remove his brain, when he looked at his watch and said, "Detective, it's lunch time." He then reaches behind him and grabbed a brown paper bag from a small table that held his tools. The sick son of a bitch pulls out a sandwich from the bag and begins to eat it while he's standing over the corpse. I looked at him for a split second in disbelief and said, "How could you eat lunch?"

He looked over at me and said, "I'm a doctor."

I stared back with contempt and shouted before walking out, "I don't care who the hell you are, you'll never autopsy me, you freak!"

Back to the Capolla homicide. It's well known that the private sanitation industry is run and controlled by the mob, at least it is in New York. His partner is Gary Corso, son of Carmine Corso. Corso Sr. is alleged to be a senior member of the Genovese crime family. His legitimate business is also in private carting, but he makes the bulk of his money from his illegal business enterprises. His last arrest dates back some fifteen years ago. He was swept up in a multi-million-dollar gambling and loansharking investigation conducted by federal and state law enforcement agencies. It's approximated that Corso's operation took in an estimated $5,000,00 a year from his illegal activities.

There was a new DA in town when I returned to work. All I knew about him was that he came from the Security Exchange Commission, was a graduate of Georgetown Law School and prosecuted some high-profile insider trading cases. Daniels had retired and the new DA appointed Larry Christopher, Chief of Detectives. Christopher, at forty-six, is tall, slim and fair skinned. His striking dark blue eyes and short cropped blond hair sets him apart from most guys his age. Larry called me earlier in the morning to tell me that DA, John Hogan called an 11:00 a.m. meeting in his office and wants me there.

I was a bit antsy and arrived for the meeting five minutes early. The uniformed police officer seated outside Hogan's office recognized me as I walked up to him. The duty officer, a big Irish American cop, glanced up from his newspaper and said, "Frank, they're expecting you. Go right in."

I was a little jittery when I walked in, not knowing what to expect. I looked around the room. Deputy Chief Achim was sitting next to ADA Falcone in front of Hogan's desk. There were also two people that I didn't recognize, in their early thirties, seated next to Falcone. The woman was a knockout. She had soft white skin tones, smartly dressed in a light blue blouse, blue jeans that defined her shapely curves, a diamond encrusted Rolex adorned her wrist and she wore black stilettos that matched her eyes. Ya know some woman just exude sexuality. It was extremely hard not to wonder what she's all about. Her companion was fair skinned, had a stocky build with blonde hair, neatly trimmed. He stood about 5' 11" inches tall, with hazel eyes that burned through you like a cattle brand. Casually dressed, in blue jeans, a creamed colored sports shirt, brown loafers and an expensive gold Rolex watch that was draped around his wrist. I couldn't help but notice that his head was bandaged with cotton gauze. It was the small spots of blood had leaked through the bandage that made it so noticeable. I wondered what his tale of woe was?

Hogan, impressive looking, in his late thirties, stands six feet, with neatly combed dirty blonde hair. Dressed conservatively in a Brooks Brothers suit, motioned to the gorgeous female and then to me and said, "Frank, I'd like you to meet Gary and his wife Dana Corso." Hogan continued in a pressing voice, "I'm sure you couldn't help but notice that Mr. Corso is wearing a bandage on his forehead. He was shot by two men wearing ski masks at his place of business in the Bronx. The men walked into the maintenance garage, brandishing pistols and began firing at him. Fortunately for Mr. Corso, he was able to dive under one of the garbage trucks, which saved his life. His partner, Lenard Capolla wasn't so lucky, he was murdered several weeks ago at his residence in New Rochelle. Since the shooting, Mr. Corso has moved his carting company from the Bronx to a facility in New Rochelle.

Assistant District Attorney Falcone jumped into the fray. "Since the Capolla homicide, the drivers of Gary's company have been threatened and assaulted on their routes. They been told to stay off the trucks or else. And now, Gary was almost killed."

Hogan, his voice assertive said, "Frank, that's where you come in."

I leaned forward in my chair, not really understanding what he meant. "Excuse me. I don't understand how I fit in with all of this? I don't work homicide, sir. I'm assigned to the narcotics squad." I knew that the powers to be were going to screw with me again.

Hogan got up from behind his desk and stood over me. "Frank, we want you to start driving one of Gary's garbage trucks. With any luck, you might find out who's behind the assaults on the drivers, the attempt on Gary's life and maybe you can find out who killed Leonard Capolla."

I'm thinking, me drive a garbage truck? That's ridiculous. What are they thinking? Just as I was trying to digest all of this, Chief Christopher interjected, looking over at the Corso's, then back at me. "We all know that the carting industry is controlled by organized crime. We also know that Gary's father is a reputed Capo in the Genovese crime family. Capolla's murder and the assault on Gary have all the earmarks of being mob related. Frank, since you've infiltrated and worked in a mob crew, DA Hogan and I both agree that you'd be a perfect fit in investigating these cases."Fuck, out of the frying pan and right back into the fire. One part of me was excited about the assignment, the other part knew firsthand that the personal toll would be enormous. The assignment had to affect my relationship with Denise. I'd have to focus all of my energy on the investigation and I knew that I won't have much left over to devote on our budding romance. This was a huge problem for me. I got a second change on life and I didn't want to lose Denise in the mix.

The Corso's were looking for a way out of the dangerous mess they were in. They desperately looked to me to throw them a lifeline. It was fait accompli, I'd be picking up garbage for Gary Corso.

"Huh, Gary, it looks like I'll be driving for you, but know that my ass is on the line. If your father finds out that I'm driving for you, it could be my life. Capisci? You gotta know that people like your father hate cops. You get my drift?"

"Yes detective." Gary said. "Mr. Hogan said that the only people who will know about your involvement with me are the people in this room."

The thought of driving a 13-ton garbage truck didn't faze me a bit. As a matter of fact, I've always loved driving big equipment. On college break, in the summer, I worked for the Town of Harrison, NY, pushing garbage into an incinerator with a bulldozer at the town dump. I figured, how hard could operating a garbage truck be. Besides, I'd be focused on locking up the people responsible for the attempt on Gary's life and killing Leonard Corso. At the end of our meeting, Chief Christopher gave Gary my fictitious personal history to place in his office personnel file. Starting on Monday, I'd be Frank Miranda again.

Chapter Thirty

Since I wouldn't start driving the garbage truck for the Corso's until Monday, I had the weekend off. Denise reserved a room at the Renaissance Providence Hotel in Rhode Island. This weekend would be as romantic as it gets. Alimony, what's left of my family and job obligations have prevented this kind of freedom. Finally, Denise had given me back a sense of normalcy in my life.

The apartment door closed behind us as we made our way down the five flights of stairs and out of the building to the rear parking lot. For the ride up to Providence, Denise was dressed casually in blue jeans and a yellow cardigan top. I wore my faithful blue jeans, white linen shirt and navy-blue sports jacket. I gave Denise a friendly peck on the cheek and a thumbs-up before putting our suitcases into the trunk of Denise's 2004, tan, Chrysler Sebring convertible. It was a warm day in June and as soon as we were settled into the car, she'd put the top down. Denise said that she wanted to drive and that was fine with me. I could sit back, relax and think that the most beautiful woman on earth liked me.

Providence is best known for its rich history, its an Italian American community, abundant with fine Italian restaurants, some of them we plan to enjoy. We arrived at the hotel at 1 p.m., the designated check-in time. A bell-boy took our luggage and showed us to room 415. The room was decorated with Early American furniture and papered in soft yellow and blue stripes. After unpacking, I called down to the concierge and asked him to recommend a moderately priced Italian restaurant for dinner. He suggested Luciano's on Atwell Avenue, just up the street from the hotel. He was able to get us an 8:00 p.m. reservation.

We wanted to see everything that the inner city of Providence had to offer. After sightseeing for an hour, visiting the trendy shops and Federalist homes that are now museums, we returned to the hotel room. Relaxed and in love, we were both on fire with sexual energy that was coursing through our bodies. Her come hither glances and natural beauty sent me into a sexual frenzy. No words were said. Our chemistry was so strong that nothing or no one in the world could stop us. It wasn't long before we had our clothes off and in the shower. I spun her around and into my arms, pressing my body into hers. As the warm water fell over our torrid bodies, I poured liquid soap into my hands and began to gently massage her entire body. She groaned wildly, screaming passionately for me to enter her. In a state of bliss, I slowly penetrated her, thrusting myself in rhythmic sync. Moaning, she mouthed, "Frankie, I love the way you make love to me. Don't ever stop making love the way you do." We continued to thrust out bodies into one other, until we couldn't stand the pleasure any longer; both of us simultaneously reached orgasm. Out of breath, we held each other as we basked in the afterglow of our love making. I don't know about Denise, but I've never experienced that kind of deep sexual connection with any other woman. From that point in time, she defined what loving someone emotionally and physically was all about.

What happened next literally blew my mind. As we were dressing for dinner, Falcone called. He told me to find a chair. "What's up Robert?"

"Are you sitting down?"

"Robert, it's my day off. We're just about to leave for dinner."

"Sorry, but you need to know that Gary Corso and an unidentified woman were shot to death early this morning in his company's waste management yard. They were found by an employee inside his Benz."

I sat on the edge of the bed trying to digest what Robert just said. Gary Corso was shot dead. It almost seemed surreal to me. Just the other day he was alive and we spoke. Now he no longer exists. The end of life; the finality of the whole thing upset me to my core. I was scheduled to begin driving for him on Monday. Now it looks like he and his company are defunct. Denise stood over me. By the look on my face, she knew that something was terribly wrong.

"Well Robert, it looks like I won't be driving for Gary? he's dead."

"Not so. From what I understand, his wife plans to run the company."

"Someone dead," she gasped. She bent down and threw her arms around me. "I hope I can be strong enough for you. I know that Helen wasn't."

That's the million-dollar question. Would she be able to handle the world I lived in? I pushed myself, trying not to let the news of Gary's murder spoil the night. It was almost eight o'clock and we had to get a move on. The romantic atmosphere had dissipated and the mood was somber as we dressed for dinner in relative silence.

We decided to walk to the restaurant, it was a short distance from the hotel. Denise turned a few heads as we walked out of the lobby into the tepid night. She wore a short white skirt, Hermes belt and light blue cotton blouse. I gotta say, for a moment, looking at her curves as we walked, it took my thoughts miles away from Gary's murder. This woman made me feel alive and excited to be alive!

We entered Luciano's, the ornate décor was similar to many of the Italian restaurants in New York. A starchy looking maître d' in his late fifties, wearing a tuxedo escorted us to our table. A white damask tablecloth covered the table and small crystal vase holding a red rose centered the top. A short time later a perky waitress came over to take our drink order. I'd calmed down and we both seemed to relax, chatting about the history of Federal Hill and its historic architecture. I loved the fact that Denise was so interested about researching the things that she didn't know about. She used Google and You-Tubed for everything. What little Denise knew of her father, she remembered him being the same way. He'd research everything. Her Aunt Margaret told her that her father would skim through the encyclopedia for information just for fun. Me personally, I don't really care that much about a lot of things because of my dyslexia. The truth be known, I have a hard time remembering things. That's why I have to focus extra hard on the task at hand, like playing the role of Frank Miranda.

In short order, the waitress placed a Chardonnay in front of Denise and a Campari and soda in front of me. She said that she'd be back in a minute to take our order. Denise reached across the table and took hold of my hand. Looking starry-eyed she said, "I really love spending time with you Frankie."

As we sipped our drinks, Denise noticed two men on the other side of the dining room pointing and staring at me. At first, she didn't say anything, but when they continued to stare, she brought it to my attention. She quickly took hold of my arm. I felt the pressure from her grip as she dug her nails into my arm. "Frankie, there are two guys sitting across from us that are staring at you." She tossed her head in their direction. I turned slightly to look at them; really not expecting to see anyone I knew. After all, we were in Rhode Island. Turning back towards Denise, I replied, "I don't recognize either of them."

Nervously, she blurted out, "Frankie, they're still staring at you. Something's wrong."

The situation was clearly upsetting Denise. She didn't know where to look or what to say next. One of the men pushed his chair back, stood and started over for our table. I was trying to place him, but I couldn't. I pulled out my 357 pistol from under my sports jacket and placed it on my lap. The guy was now standing by my chair. He was nicely dressed in beige slacks and a black sports jacket, looked to be an Italian American and in his late thirties. Denise sat there frozen in fear, staring up at the guy. I was waiting for the shit to hit the fan. As my mind raced, I'm thinking maybe I've locked the guy up? Maybe he wants to get even with me for something he thinks I did? My adrenaline kicked in, big time, I was on overdrive and prepared for what came next.

"Frank, you don't recognize me, do you?"

"No Pal," I said, as I tensed up, my hand squarely on the butt of my pistol. "I don't know who the hell you are. Now get out of my face. I'm trying to have dinner."

Denise sat there scared to death. She tried to mumble something, but nothing clear enough out of her mouth. I stood up, looked the guy directly in his eyes, we were so close that I could smell wine on his breath. He could clearly see my hand on the grip of my gun. The motherfucker didn't flinch. He replied aggressively, "Frank, you should remember me, I'm Mickey Calise's nephew, Joey. You put me in jail a while back. I came over to say hello. And by the way, I own the restaurant; enjoy the rest of your dinner." I'm thinking, there's no place I can escape to without these knuckleheads popping up.

"Now I remember you." I barked. "I used to drop off my numbers work to you in your uncle Nino's barber shop. Joey, you've put on a few pounds since I last saw you. I guess the food in the joint agrees with you."

Grinning he replied, "Yeah, prison will do that to you. Your dinners are on me tonight."

You can imagine, how upset Denise was. Trembling and almost in tears she said, "Frankie, I want to leave. Please take me back to the hotel." Since our dinners hadn't arrived, I threw a few bucks on the table to pay for our drinks. I eyed Joey as we left the dining room and headed for the restaurant's front door. On the way back to the hotel Denise was a nervous wreck. She kept looking behind us, for fear that Joey would follow us out and shoot us. "Frankie," she gasped. "I'm so scared. What just happened in there? Are we going to be okay?"

"Yes, we're going to be fine. Try and calm down." In all honesty, I didn't know if we were gonna be okay. Joey was a hot head and a loose cannon. As we hurried into the lobby, she said, "Frankie, please take me home. I'm not used to this. I don't know if I'll ever get used to it."

We packed immediately. The night clerk asked why we were leaving? Denise rolled her eyes at the clerk and spat out, "We're just leaving! Thank you!"

Chapter Thirty-one

The murdered girlfriend of Gary Corso was identified as Clare Iverson. She was twenty-eight and danced for a living in one of the hotels in Las Vegas. Clare was gorgeous, tall, blonde and very shapely. At nineteen, Clare won the title of Miss Connecticut just two years ago. She relocated to California and tried her hand at acting for a while, then made her way to Vegas to become a showgirl. How she ended up dying with Gary Corso is a mystery.

When Gary was shot in the Bronx, he began to carry an unlicensed 38 caliber pistol. Two New Rochelle Detectives, Straub and Barry investigated the murder of Lenard Capolla, Gary's business partner and decided to pay Gary a visit at his yard in New Rochelle. From what I later found out later, by charging him with an illegal handgun, their strategy was to pressure him into divulging information about his partner's homicide.

Bill Barry, a portly Irishman, having sharp blue eyes, in his early fifties and Donald Straub, a rather tall and slim man, in his mid-forties, are two seasoned detectives with stone cold personalities and no compassion for anyone. Like many cops, they find their compassion for people in a good bottle of whiskey. As I said, they stopped by Gary's office to speak to him about Lenard's murder and just happened to notice the butt of a handgun protruding from Gary's waist. Straub pointed to the pistol and asked, "Gary, you have a permit for that gun?"

When questioned in depth by the detectives, he told them that he didn't have a permit for the gun and bought it on the street to defend himself. They arrested him on the spot, thinking that now they had some leverage to force him to cooperate. They were wrong, dead wrong. Gary continued to insist that he knew nothing about Lenny's murder and by taking the gun, they were leaving him defenseless. He was right. A few days after Gary's arrest, he and Clare Iverson were gunned down in Gary's car. If they had looked the other way, Gary and Claire just might still be alive today.

The killings have Mafia written all over them. I never thought for a moment that the murders were the result of a love triangle. I often wondered if Dana Corso knew that Gary even had a mistress, then again, of course she had to know. The world Gary lived in, having a girlfriend is common thing. As it turned out, Dana got a cool three million dollars from Gary's life insurance policy taken out just months before his murder. This was certainly a motive for murder. According to Dana, Gary's father Carmine, offered to buy the business back from her, but Dana decided that she didn't want to sell.

Like it or not, I'd be driving a garbage truck for Dana. Driving a truck for a private sanitation company was all too new for me. But honestly, I loved challenge. As a kid growing up, I always had to prove myself because of my disability. I had to show people that I was as smart as everyone else. It was a must that I excelled at everything that I did, whether on the high school football team, baseball team. Classwork was a different story. My desire to succeed served me well as an undercover cop. It was a love/hate feeling for my work. My mind never stopped running; my head resting on my pillow was no relief. Tomorrow was always a new challenge that my mind couldn't resist. I never knew how things were going to turn the next day. I'd shut off the lights and play out every scenario in my head; hour after hour, until I'd eventually drift off to sleep.

Dana asked Louis Fuganza, aka Nutsey to ride along with me on the truck to work the hopper at the rear of the truck. He controled pushing the garbage into the main body. Nutsey's in his early forties with forearms like a tree trunk. I shit you not, he looks just like Popeye. He's barreled chested like Popeye, keeps his light brown hair in ponytail and wears a gray skullcap. The only thing missing is a corncob pipe and a girlfriend named Olive Oil. I learned that he's a simple man who doesn't expect much out of life. He reminded me of one of my father's brothers, Rocky, who saw everything as either black or white. There were never any gray areas in his life to make his decisions difficult. Come to find out, Nutsey had a heart of gold and would help you if he could.

Then there was Jimmy Newcomb the office manager. He's a mean-spirited dwarf with a huge temper. The first time I laid eyes on him, he was slovenly dressed in overalls, a dirty sweatshirt and wearing work boots. In his early thirties, his greasy brown hair looked like it needed a good washing. The upside of it all, is that I knew that I had to get along with the little man if I wanted to get anywhere with the murder investigations. It was after 3:00 a.m. and pitch black outside when I drove into the yard and parked alongside the other driver's cars. As I locked my car, I noticed one of the drivers standing by his truck, smoking a cigarette. I walked over and introduced myself as a new driver starting today. We shook hands. "I'm Dave Cook. Good luck Miranda. You're gonna need it by the way things have been going around here."

"What do ya mean?" I knew very well what he was talking about, but I didn't dare let on.

"You'll find out soon enough."

Cook, a large man, about 6 foot-five, looked to be in his early sixties and appeared that the hard road of life had taken its toll on him.

"You'd better get your ass up to the second floor, you're late." He pointed to a two-story red-faced building across the parking lot. "See ya later," he said as I walked away.

It was showtime and I was ready to rock and roll. I could feel my heart pounding in my chest. I had to make myself believe that I could pull this assignment off. And yes, the reality of picking up tons of garbage everyday had finally sunken in. I had to make the people at C&C Carting believe that I'd driven a garbage truck before.

Newcomb was standing with his back towards me when I walked into his office. When he heard the door open, he turned around and looked up. His blue eyes seemed to burrow through me as he moved toward me, clenching his tiny fists. "You're fuckin' late Miranda! We start at three, not 3:15! Got it Frank!" I didn't say a word. I nodded my head in agreement. I'd developed a knack of instantly sizing up a person, so I kept my cool. There was something about him that I didn't like. I knew from looking into his eyes that the little prick was dangerous. I also knew that there would be a day of reckoning between us. It's a personal thing with me. I can't stand it when someone talks down to me or his tone is rough. It ignites the fire already burning inside of me. I can't suppress it until I strike back at the inciter. I noticed a man sitting on an old, weathered couch behind Jimmy's beat-up oak desk. He was sitting there, squirming in his overalls and looked like he wanted to be somewhere else. I can't say that I could blame him.

"Uh, I'm sorry Jimmy, it won't happen again."

The little bastard gave me a cold stare and said, "Only my friends call me by my first name. You're not my friend Miranda."

"Yes sir, Mr. Newcomb, I got it."

Jimmy grabbed a half-smoked cigar from a dirty ashtray on his desk, lit it, rolled it to one side of his mouth, took a large drag then slowly blew out the smoke, blowing it straight into my face. Then he raised his squeaky voice and said, "It's late! Now you and Nutsey get to work and get the fuck out of my office!"

We left the office and hurried down the wrought iron stairs to the yard. It's funny what goes through your mind when you're under stress. I remembered when I was about 12 years old my folks left the car keys to the Chevy on the kitchen windowsill. It was early in the day and I'd just gotten home from school. Being ballsy, I thought, what the hell I'll take the car for a joy ride. The only caveat was that I'd forgotten that my grandfather, Guarino was home. After I'd taken the keys, I guess he'd gone into the kitchen for something and notice that the keys to the car were gone. He knew I'd come home from school and must have taken them. He ran to the front door, looked out to see as I unlocked the car door and jumped in. He must have been shouting for me to get out of the car, but I didn't hear him. I shoved the key into the ignition and started the car. Well, my foot must have hit the gas pedal a little too hard and the car bolted out diagonally, across the street, through the neighbor's hedge and ended up in his tomato garden. To my misfortune, the neighbor happened to be home. He came running out of his house holding his head and screaming, "Frankie, what have you done! What have you done? My tomatoes!"

My grandfather rushed out of the house. When he saw that the family car had crashed through the neighbor's hedge and saw that the car landed in Mr. Vitullo's tomato garden, he went absolutely nuts. My grandfather ran across the street, saw me sitting in the driver's seat trying to back it out of the garden. The more I accelerated the engine, the more the wheels spun, sending the car deeper and deeper into the soft dirt. My grandpa was frantic. In his broken-English, he yelled, "Frankie, you, no-a-good-a, kid. When you father come-a home, he's-a gonna kick you ass! He was so animated, jumping up and down, screaming at the top of his lungs. It was a given that the car had to be towed out of the garden. We all stood there and watched the car, tires mid-deep in dirt, as it was dragged from the garden by the tow truck. All the while my grandfather is ranting on, "I can't-a wait. When you fada come-a-home, you-son-of-a- bitch, he's gonna kick your ass!"

He was right on the money. As soon as my dad walked into the house, my grandfather gave him a blow-by-blow account of the sorry event. I can still feel the strikes on my ass from my dad's leather belt. Unfortunate as it is, it seems that I always had to learn the hard way. Looking back on it now, what I did was funny. Ya know, you gotta have a sense of humor to get by in this crazy world.

Chapter Thirty-two

Nutsey was antsy as we hurried to the truck. "Miranda, we got 20 stops to make, let's get going."

I began to sweat as we pulled our way up into the cab of the five-speed standard shift Mack garbage truck. Beads of sweat began to build up on my forehead. I knew that I had to tell Nutsey that I'd never driven a garbage truck in my life and I needed his help to get by. If he didn't help me, my involvement in this investigation could end here and now. I couldn't figure out, for the life of me, how the people in my office thought that I could drive a garbage truck without training. My lack of experience could have blown the investigation. I started the truck and pushed the gear shift into first gear, grinding the gears as it engaged. Fuckin' Nutsey looked at me like I had two heads. I slowly drove out of the lot. I glanced over to where my car was parked, thinking that's where Gary and his girlfriend were probably shot dead.

Newcomb was still on my mind as I drove onto 4th Street, but for now, I had more pressing things to think about, like driving this damn truck. I looked over at Nutsey to get a better feel for the guy. He appeared to be the nervous sort, constantly fidgeting with his body. In a strained gruff voice Nutsey muttered, "C'mon Miranda, at the rate we're goin', it'll take us all day." Halfway up the block, I pulled the truck to the curb. I knew I couldn't pull this off without his help. We were picking up commercial stops. Garbage containers that held from 10 to 50 yards of garbage. I figured, what the hell, this was as good a time as any to tell Nutsey that I've never driven a garbage truck in my life.

"Nutsey, I've never driven a garbage truck before. I saw the add in the paper for a driver and took the job because I needed the money."

The guy looked like he was going to pass out. His lips were moving but no words were coming out. Finally, he was able to speak. "You say what?" His face turned the color of mud. He looked like his circulatory system was about to shut down. He screamed, "Whoa, what d' ya mean ya never drove a garbage truck?"

"Look, Nutsey, if you don't help me, I'm fucked. I'm on the balls of my ass and need to eat and pay my rent."

He stared out the window shaking his head for a minute. Thankfully, his conscience took over. He said shaking his head, "Okay Miranda, I'll help you, but it ain't gonna be easy."

Before I could operate the truck, I hit everything but a human being. Banks, overpasses, florescent lights that hung over the gas pumps at a local gas station. It got so bad that I had to down a half bottle of Cognac before I had the courage to start the truck in the morning.

With the insurance claims mounting, Shorty Newcomb wanted my head on a silver platter. The truth be known, I wanted off the truck more than he did. Worst of it all was that I wasn't getting any closer to solving the homicides. Days turned into months. It's a sure bet that the people responsible for the homicides were hell bent on taking over C&C Carting. I prayed that an attempt would be made to stop my truck on the route, but it never happened. I've been trying to illicit information about the homicides from Nutsey and the other drivers, but they refused to talk about it, probably out of fear of reprisal.

It came to a head one day when Newcomb and I went at it. The little bastard was irate over me demolishing a delivery guys hatch back as he delivered pastries to one of his stops. I gotta say, I roughed the little toad up pretty bad.

Carmine Corso, who happened to be in the office chatting with Dana, heard the commotion, calmly walked out of the office and down the steps to the yard. I had to laugh; he was no stranger to violence. All he said when he walked over, directing his comment to the drivers, who had witnessed the incident, "Get Jimmy into the office." He then looked at me and said,

"You're costing my daughter-in-law a fortune, you better get your act together." My effort in the investigation was going nowhere and everyone in my office knew it. Furthermore, the wise guys who were trying to take over Dana's company were relentless. They torched two of Dana's garbage trucks in the early in the morning hours. The padlock on the front gate was cut. This was typical of organized crime. That was their M.O. (modus operandi), torching trucks, forcing small mom and pop companies to relinquish their ownership. But this didn't make any sense to me. Carmine Corso is a Capo in the Genovese crime family. I would think that he would protect his daughter-in-law's interest in her company. Something was going on with Carmine and I needed to find out what it was. I 'd remembered that he initially offered to buy the company back when his son was murdered, but at the time, she didn't want to sell. Maybe now, she'll have second thoughts. Her drivers were quitting and her trucks were being burned. This infuriated me. I've always been for the underdog. In my eyes that's what Dana was, even though she was a wealthy woman, Dana was going up against the mob and she didn't stand a chance. I guess that everyone knew it but her.

On one of the last days driving for Dana, things really started to go south. I arrived back at the yard after finishing my route and noticed an unmarked police car parked behind one of the garbage trucks. After filling the truck with diesel fuel, I parked it the garage. As Nutsey walked to his car to leave, I was about to do the same thing when Newcomb ran out of the office, got into his late model, baby blue, Cadillac Eldorado and sped out of the yard like the devil was chasing him.

There was definitely something going on in the office. As usual, I wasn't gonna let it go. Before heading up to the office, I tucked my 9mm under the front seat of my car. As it turned out, it was a good thing I did. I heard voices coming from the office. A male voice resounded above the rest. "You know a lot more than you're telling us!"

I knew Dana's voice. She cried out, "No, I don't! Please believe me!"

I knocked, then opened the door to see what the commotion was about. Dana was seated on the couch with a large male hovering over her. "That's bullshit, that's bullshit!" Another man stood off to the side, his arms crossed, looking like he was going to bite someone's head off. At that moment, I had a flash back of being bullied as a kid because of my dyslexia and that really set me off. I was outraged by what I saw. I lost it, shouting, "What's going on? What the fuck do think you're going? Leave the woman alone!" I found out later that they were New Rochelle Detectives Straub and Barry. They were trying to pressure Dana into talking about her husband's murder. What enraged me even more was that I believed that these two cowboys were responsible for getting Gary killed. Straub, his face distorted with anger, rushed me. He grabbed me by the arms, turned me around then cranking my arm up at a right angle and forced it up to my shoulder blade. Detective Barry was right behind him. They both threw me up against the wall, as Straub drew his pistol and stuck the barrel up against my temple yelling, "Get up against the wall and don't move!" The guy's gun was cocked as he held the gun on my head. From the corner of my eye, his forefinger resting on the trigger. I hollered, "I'm against the wall. Do you want me to go up or down? I'll do whatever you say, but please take the gun off of my head." My life could have very well ended. I thought, I'd hate to have my life end from a bullet from another cop.

I'm not sure if he realized what he was doing, but after a few seconds, he holstered his pistol. Detective Barry then systematically patted me down for weapons. After I'd been roughed up, Straub released his hold and identified themselves as New Rochelle detectives. Forcefully, Straub then removed my wallet and tossed it on Newcomb's desk. Dana watched all this take place. She kept spouting "Leave him alone! He hasn't done anything!" Barry thumbed through my wallet. Remember, I've been through this act before. He removed my driver's license and social security card, writing my personal information down on a 3 x 5 note pad. Then, Straub threw my license back in my face. "Next time Miranda, mind your business," Straub growled. They turned to Dana before walking out. Detective Barry snarled, "We'll be back."

It wasn't long after my run in with Barry and Straub that my bosses felt that the investigation had turned cold and I was taken off the case. Mafia killings are hard to solve and this one was no exception. Unless there were some breaking developments in the case, the investigation was shelved. But I knew that I would never let it go. I've invested too much of myself into solving the murders, besides, I had some scores to settle.

Chapter Thirty-three

Every case I've worked has laid the foundation for my next investigation. More or less, I've known what to expect and how to react to a lot of uncomfortable situations. Between cases, I get a chance to hang out in the squad room and recharge my batteries. But I gotta say, with the exception of a few other cops like me, many of the detectives in the squad don't understand me and keep their distance.

On my second day back, my desk phone rang. It was my cousin Tommy's wife Anna. She was crying hysterically. "Anna, what's wrong? Calm down." She told me that Tommy had been shot while closing his gym on White Plains Road in the Bronx. As she spoke to me, I could hear their two young kids crying. Anna, through her tears, told me that Tommy was in the intensive care unit at Montefiore Medical Center in the Bronx, undergoing surgery. That set me back on my heels. My cousin being shot and his wife and kids crying hysterically, tore me up inside. There was no way I was going to let this go. I knew that I had to find this mutt so he could pay for what he did.

The Bronx cops told me that the guy who shot my cousin was Alex Shivone. He's a leg breaker for a mob guy, by the name of Little Augie Pisano. Tommy's shooting looked like a mob hit that failed. Shivone is an ex-boxer, who's street name is Crazy Alex. He's been shaking down my cousin for free gym membership and helping himself to health food bars and drinks. But Tommy had the balls to stand up to him, that's what got him shot. Unfortunately for my cousin, he experienced firsthand, the world I have to deal with. People like my cousin can't escape the dirt that lives among us. Thank God for the police, we're shit extractors. We remove the shit-bags who plague our society.

Anna, crying into the phone was inconsolable. "Anna is he gonna be okay?"

"Frankie, the bullet passed through his side. He's lost a lot of blood, but the doctors say that he's gotta a good chance to live."

I breathed a little easier. "That's good."

"I'm worried Frankie. Shivone is out there. I'm afraid that he might come after me and the kids."

I knew that Alex was in the wind. But the fact remained, Tommy would testify against him. With Tommy out of the way, there was no case against Alex. I knew guys like Alex, he was definitely coming after my cousin.

Chapter Thirty-four

It was a Bronx case, so I planned to hunt for Alex Shivone on my own time. When I locate him and I will, I'll asked Nulligan and Angel Serano for their help. I can always count on these two guys to watch my back. They've been tested like tempered steel. Angel and his family emigrated from Puerto Rico when he was ten years old. He knows the ins and outs of life on the street. Angel grew up in the South Bronx, is bilingual and is one of the most capable cops I know. Unfortunately for me, he happened to be away on military leave. So, it was going to be Nulligan and me. I asked Joe Nulligan to meet me at Jake's Bar & Grill to talk things through.

Nulligan's girlfriend Jessica was tending bar when I walked in. Jess is young, beautiful, energetic and in her mid-twenties. They met a few years ago and became inseparable. They've finally moved in together last year. She rents an apartment on Shore Road in New Rochelle. She's tall, flowing black hair, dark blues eye and has a body to kill for. I've always wondered why girls like Jessica and Denise go for blue collar guys like Joe and I. Maybe it's their need for adventure.

I ordered a Guinness and took it with me into the dining room where Joe was sitting in a booth nursing a beer. I sat down and laid everything out for Joe. Joe took a gulp of his beer and was on board right away. He knew how important it was for me to find Shivone. "Frankie, whatever it takes, we'll find him."

Our informants were key. They just might know of Alex's whereabouts. Our conversation, for the most part was guarded. Ya never know who's in earshot. After a few beers, Joe and I were feeling no pain. We'd had several refills when my cousin Tommy called my cell phone. He'd been out of the hospital for a few days and home recuperating. He said that Anna is scared to death for him and the kids. He just found a brick that had been thrown through the front windshield of his car, with a note attached. The note, printed in bold black letters, said that he had better not testify against him or he wouldn't live to see his next birthday.
"Cuz, you gotta find him. I'm afraid for my family."

"Tommy, hang tight. I'm goin' to the 47th precinct and see what they're doin' about finding the dirt bag."

An hour later, I walked into the precinct on Laconia Avenue. I identified myself to the desk sergeant and asked to speak to the detectives on duty. He summoned a patrolman to escort me to the squad detectives on the second floor. When I walked in, a detective was sitting at his desk, with a cigarette hanging out of the side of his mouth, banging away on his computer. There was a large holding cell with some disheveled drugged up guy sitting on a steel bunk, holding his head in his hands. He looked like he'd been through the mill and the worst was yet to come.

The detective, a black male in his forties, stopped what he was doing and asked if he could help me. I told him who I was and that I was here about the Shivone case. I said that the complainant in the case was my cousin Tommy Santorsola. "You understand that I have a personal interest in the case. Have you made any headway in finding Shivone?

The detective was blunt. He said that the squad was so overwhelmed with homicides that they back burnered the Santorsola case. I brought Detective Williams up to speed, informing him that Shivone had just threatened my cousin. He said that if my cousin testifies there would be deadly consequences. He'd thrown a brick through the windshield of his car, with a note attached. I then asked to see the bagged evidence relating to the case. What the detective said next, floored me. He said that after shooting Tommy, Alex had dropped a 25-caliber automatic at the scene, before he got into his car and sped away. We took it into evidence, but it's nowhere to be found.

"What the fuck? You can't find it?" I'm thinking, maybe Shivone got to the cops and made the case go away. I shook my head. "What other evidence do you have? Any witnesses besides my cousin?"

"It was early morning. There were no witnesses. Your cousin is it."

Shivone is on the run. Detective, Alex is out on bail on another case. Alex broke his girlfriend's arm in a domestic dispute two weeks ago. He's charged with 2nd degree assault, but he made bail."

"My cousin can't remember what make car Alex drove up in. Would you know what he drives?"

"Detective Williams got up and walked over to a filing cabinet in the corner of the room. Thumbing through it, he pulled out a manila folder. Glancing at the reports, he said, "He's known to drive a late model Lincoln Continental."

The car that Shivone drives resonated with me. I had an old informant that I remembered worked at a Lincoln dealership in South Yonkers. I thought that he would be a good guy to talk to. Once back at the office, I picked up my desk phone, dialed the dealership and asked for him. The receptionist connected me to his office. He was a bit taken aback when he got on the phone. "Frank, it's been a long time. What's up?"

"Alex Shivone is what's up. What can you tell me about him?"

"How did you know that he rented a car from me?"

I couldn't fuckin' believe it, there is a God. Never mind slick, I want his current address and give me everything thing off his rental agreement."

"But, Frank.....He can't know...."

"You let me worry about Alex. Give me everything!"

"C' mon Bob, read the freakin' rental agreement."

"Okay, Okay! A few months ago, he leased another late model Lincoln Continental, color black, NY Registration, 1234 XYX."

"What's his address on the lease?"

The tension in Bob's voice was unmistakable. "He's rented a section eight, studio apartment in the Roger Smith Hotel in White Plains."

Section eight folks are low-income families, usually on government assistance. I was chomping at the bit to get this motherfucker and put an end to his reign of terror. We're soon going to have a meeting of the minds. Now all I needed was his mug shot and a copy of the warrant for his arrest to get the show on the road.

Chapter Thirty-five

It was after midnight when Joe and I walked into the run down, dark and depressing hotel. The night clerk, an Asian man in his late fifties, looked a little worn for wear. He wore a tattered black cardigan sweater and gray slacks with coffee stains all over them. He was just another victim of the hard road of life. When he looked up and realized that Joe and I were standing in front of him, he peered over his eyeglasses that hung at the end of his nose and said, "Can I help you?" From his worried expression, he knew that we weren't there to rent a room. The poor bastard was right. We were here for Crazy Alex.

I flipped a photo of Alex's picture in front of him. Damn, my juices were pumping, I couldn't wait to see his face when I stuck my gun in it. Joe, then popped out his shield and literally shoved it into the guys face. "Police, is this guy staying here?" The clerk, swallowed hard, looked at Joe for a second, then back at me and said, "He just walked in a few minutes ago."

At that moment, all I could think about was locking Alex up. The thought of notifying the local police department never entered my mind. Slamming my hand on the desk, I demanded, "What's his room number slick?"

The clerk fumbling for words replied, "Room 201. He just took the elevator up to the room."

"Yo," I railed, "give me the pass key! And don't think about calling him!"

The squint-eyed weasel nodded and squealed,

"No, no, I won't call."

I could feel his beady eyes follow us to the elevator. We took it to the second floor. Joe and I were silent on the ride up. Every cop knows fear, managing it is the hard part. I knew instinctively that we were both thinking that Alex might not want to cooperate and decide to go the hard way. If that was the case, the mutt would end up in a body bag and that was fine with me.

I can't say that I wasn't a little uneasy as we walked up the hallway to room 201. We sort of read each other's mind as we glanced over at each other before I slid the pass key into the door lock. I turned the doorknob and slowly opened the door. Pushing the door open, we rushed into the dimly lit suite, both yelling, "Police, police!" Scanning the room for Alex our training kicked in. We were reacting to a fluid situation.

A key ring of keys and a wallet were lying on an old beat-up dresser. I was drawn to a light coming from under the bathroom door. The rush was intoxicating. Alex shooting my cousin as he opened his gym was flashing before my eyes. I was viewing it like a movie. Joe slowly inched his way to the bathroom door, grabbed the doorknob and tried to open it. It was locked and the shower was running. Nulligan yelled out "Alex, police," and threw his shoulder into the door. The door exploded into the bathroom. Alex was naked, cowering down between the bathtub and the commode. There was a small caliber, semi-automatic pistol lying on top of toilet's water tank. I was riveted on Alex's hands. His eyes were darting back and forth between me and the gun. By the way he looked back at me, I felt that he was contemplating making a play for the gun. "Come on Alex, go for the gun," I screamed. Things were happening so fast that it was dreamlike. My finger resting on the trigger, about to light him up and dispatch him to a better place if he made a play for the gun. But what happened next confused me. Alex cried out, "Please don't shoot me, please don't shoot me,"and was begging for mercy.

I shrieked, "Just like you didn't shoot my cousin Tommy! You fucking coward!"

Joe moved toward Alex and secured the gun on the toilet tank, shoving it into his back pocket. He then grabbed Alex and yanked him up by his hair, forced his arms behind his back and cuffed him. At this point, Joe and I dragged Alex out of the bathroom to dress. We walked this poor excuse for a human being to the elevator and took him down to the lobby. When the elevator doors opened, the desk clerk tried to hide as we walked him out of the hotel in handcuffs. Alex was then transported to the 47th precinct for processing on his outstanding warrant. He'll be arraigned tomorrow morning in Bronx criminal court.

I was sitting in the back of the Bronx County Court as Alex, shackled, was brought into the courtroom. He was seated alongside six other prisoners at the Defendant's table. The bailiff called Shivone's case about 9:30 a.m. He stood before the bench with his attorney, Martin Richardson. Richardson primarily defends wise guys. The judge read the charge of 2nd degree attempted murder. Of course, he plead not guilty. The Assistant District Attorney, Robert Collier asked that no bail be set because Alex is a flight risk. From what Detective Williams told me of Alex's criminal history, he's already out on bail on an assault charge and not entitled to bail by New York statute. I sat on the edge of my seat knowing full well that Alex's bail application would be denied. New York State law states that if a defendant has been charged with a felony in another case and is out on bail, he is not entitled to bail for a second felony committed. I waited with bated breath for the Judges to spit it out, "bail denied!"

But, Judge Blais set Alex's bail at $100,000. I waited for the ADA Collier to object, but he didn't. I thought that the judge would have had Alex's record of arrest in front of him and knew that he wasn't entitled to bail. Apparently, he dropped the ball and didn't run a criminal history on Alex.
There was no way I was going to let Alex walk out of the courtroom. I jumped up, my police shield swinging from my neck and hastily approached the bench. Standing before the judge, I turned to Collier and said, "Shivone is not entitled to bail. He's out on bail on another felony charge in the Bronx."

"Are you sure?" Collier asked.

"Yes sir." I spat out.

Collier immediately asked one of the court officers to have a file 15 run on Shivone. The judge called a short recess while we waited for the results of the criminal history check. Alex sat at the defense table, red faced and seething. It wasn't long before the officer returned with the file 15 and handed it to ADA Collier. He approached the bench and pointed out to the judge that Alex had been arrested and charged with assaulting his girlfriend, just a few weeks ago. Judge Blais banged the gavel on the sound block and said, "bail denied! Mr. Shivone you are to be remanded to Rikers Island for future court appearances."

As the court officers were about to escort Alex out of the courtroom to a holding cell in the back, Alex stopped a few feet away from me and said, "Detective Santorsola I'll be seeing you." He then spat in my face. I lunged at him, but a few of the court officers stepped between us. As he was led away, I yelled out to him, "Alex, I'll put another nail in your coffin you miserable son of a bitch!" Damn, I wished that Alex went for his gun last night. He'd be a bad memory right now, but that wasn't the case. Alex would have his day in court and go through the criminal justice system. My cousin Tommy would have to testify if he wanted this dirt-bag off of the street.

A few weeks pasted since Alex's arrest and things had calmed down. I happened to be in the office when my desk phone rang. It was a collect call from from Rikers Island. Alex Shivone was on the line. Reluctantly I accepted the call.

"Alex, what do you want?" I snapped.

"Detective Santorsola, if you help me get out of the mess I'm in, I'll help you out with some good information."

What the scumbag just said made my blood boil. "Alex, like I told you in the courtroom, the only thing I want to do is to drive another nail into your coffin!" I slammed the phone down.

Chapter Thirty-six

Alex was almost a memory. He was going to be prosecuted and probably spend a lot of years behind bars. What happened next was a real mind blower. A few weeks after Alex's arrest, my squad commander, Captain John Matthews, a rather large do-nothing cop, told me that Chief Christopher wanted to see me in his office right away. I asked him what it was about, but he wouldn't say. I wasn't too worried because I hadn't done anything wrong, that I could think of. Besides, the Chief is a super guy and a fair man. We both took the elevator up to the fifth floor. Christopher's assistant, Liz, young and pretty, with long brown hair that bounced below her shoulders when she moved, told us to go right in. "The Chief is waiting for you."

As soon as we entered his office, he motioned for us to pull up a chair in front of his desk. I sat there a bit apprehensive and wondering what was going on. I looked over at Matthews, who had no facial expression and focused on what the Chief was about to say.

The Chief put down his coffee and got right to it. "Frank, this is a bit awkward, but I have to ask where you were last night?"

"Why Chief?"

"Just please answer me. Where were you?"

"I was home with Denise."

"All night?"

"Yes, why?"

Christopher, leaned forward, his eyes centered on mine and said, "Somehow, Alex Shivone was let out on bail. His bail was posted yesterday afternoon and he was shot to death late last night."

The chief continued, "His body was dumped in the parking lot of Saint Joseph's Seminary in Yonkers. The newspaper clipping of his arrest by you and Nulligan was found tucked into the breast pocket of his sports jacket."

Shit, I sat there frozen. My mouth hung open, thinking, maybe Little Augie Pisano thought that Alex was becoming a liability and took care of business.

"Frank, I gotta ask. Do you know anything about his murder?"

"Chief! Fuck no! I don't know anything about it, but I'm glad the scumbag is dead!" Matthews, uncomfortable, his arms crossed, sat there listening intently to what I had to say.

"Okay Frank. You're on record now. I had to ask. Captain Matthews will follow up with a call to Denise to verify your alibi. You can go back to the squad room."

I couldn't believe that the Chief asked if I had anything to do with Alex's murder. You would think that he and the rest of the bosses would know who I was by now. I'm on the right side of the criminal justice system. Like my father said many times, never dishonor our family name. It's something to be proud of. As for Alex, it's possible that he stepped on the wrong people's toes and it got him killed. One thing is for sure, my cousin Tommy and his family won't have to worry about that guy any longer.

Chapter Thirty-seven

I was exhausted from the everyday grind, everyone in the squad knew it but me. It was time to take me off the streets for a while. Chief Christopher summoned me to his office. As soon as I walked in, he smiled and asked me to have a seat. Christopher was understanding and gracious. "Frank, I asked to see you because I feel that you need a break from working the street. The change of pace will do you good. You're going to be assigned to a wiretap case that our office is undertaking. It's a money laundering case that the Organized Crime Squad will manage. You'll be reviewing the tape recordings to make sure that the detectives manning the wire are adhering to the minimization requirements prescribed by law." I thought about it for a second and welcomed the change.

"Who's the target Chief?"

"The target is Dante Malatesta, a Genovese soldier."

"Huh, minimization requirements?"

"Frank, we are not allowed to record privileged conversations, which include conversations between the target and his wife, lawyer, priest or minister, doctor, psychologist or psychiatrist. If any of these conversations are recorded, it could jeopardize the investigation if or when the case goes to trial."

After working and socializing with these guys for almost six years, listening to them on a wire, after the fact, was a welcome change. It actually gave me a new perspective on how they have affected me.

Over a few months, I'd listened to hundreds of hours of Dante Malatesta and his cronies discussing their criminal business, which I gotta say I was very familiar with. One of Dante's biggest concerns was laundering his money and funneling it back into legitimate businesses like restaurants and private carting owned by the Genovese crime family. The fruits of the wire paid off. Dante spoke almost daily with a guy from Fort Worth Texas, Spencer Johnstone. Johnstone washed Dante's dirty money. Every few weeks, Malatesta would have a courier drive a rented car to Fort Worth and deliver between $500,000 and $800,000 for cleaning. Johnston would then deposit the money into Banco National in Mexico City and have it exchanged for pesos. The laundered money was then wired to a phony mortgage company in New York City for legitimate use. Guys like Malatesta are brilliant. If they had chosen the corporate world to work in, they could have run a large successful corporation.

Malatesta's money launderer Spencer Johnstone is a wiry six-footer, who has no criminal history. He lives with his wife Maureen Sullivan Johnstone in the suburbs of Fort Worth. He owns and runs a company that creates software for corporate and small businesses. A call was intercepted between Johnston and Malatesta. Spencer told Dante that he'd developed a software program that will computerize illegal gambling records. The illegal bets collected, whether sports or number bets are manually entered into the computer program. After all the daily bets have been taken, the sheet writer, working in a wire room, forwards them to a compatible computer, in an undisclosed location to safeguard them from police seizure. This program keeps track of the daily winning numbers and sporting events, odds on each event, the bettor's names, the runner who took the bet, monies wagered, commission earned, money won and lost and the pay outs. The best feature of the system is that the daily records are downloaded to Mexico City for safe keeping. The cost of outfitting each of Malatesta's wire rooms is $25,000 and a monthly service fee of $500. This was something that Dante was interested in, but he would have to take the idea to his higher-ups.

The courier, Patrick Johns is a burly Irishman with a pot-marked face. At 6' 1", Pat's muscular with an intimidating demeanor. His rap sheet reads like "Who's Who" in organized crime. He's been arrested and convicted of drug smuggling, extortion, labor racketeering, assault to cause bodily injury, loansharking, illegal gambling, burglary and witness tampering. He has been implicated in several murders, but there wasn't enough evidence to charge him. Johns has spent a total of thirty of his 61 years on earth in either state or federal prison. In the 1970's and 80's, according to the law enforcement sources, Johns was a member of "The Westies," an infamous Irish American gang that terrorized the business owners of Hell's Kitchen, an area located on Manhattan's West Side. The gang was directly tied to the Gambino Crime Family, at the time, run by Big Paul Castellano. Their handy work included extortion and contract killings.

Since Johns release from prison, he has successfully stayed below law enforcement's radar until now. We learned from the wire that Johns failed to make a scheduled delivery of $800,000. Dante hired a former disgraced NYPD detective to track Johns' cell phone activity and locate his whereabouts. Jack Shaw was forced to resign at an early age from the NYPD for shaking down drug dealers and prostitutes. Now working as a private investigator, he's able to track cell phone calls from a contact in the phone company. In one conversation, Dante was heard telling Johnston that he's sending Peter Esposito find Johns, torture him until he gets his money back and then kill him.

Although I wasn't working on the street at the time, just by listening to the conversations dug up old wounds. The kind that keeps you up at night. It's like having a recurring nightmare every night. When I do fall asleep, I dream about casing Malatesta in an endless alleyway, never able to catch and arrest him. And there's always another low life to add to the mix, Peter Esposito. His dossier reflected that he's a brutish misfit. Now in his mid-fifties, he's been locked up for assault with a deadly weapon and grand larceny.

The case was breaking wide open and I was back on the street. Joe Nulligan and I were tasked to find Patrick Johns before Pete Esposito did. The strategy was to convince Johnstone to cooperate with my office or face charges of money laundering and conspiracy to commit murder. We were dispatched to Texas to offer Johnstone a way out of the mess he created. For his cooperation, it was no jail time and witness protection for him and his family.

When Joe and I braced Johnstone, it was a no-brainier for him. He wanted no part of a homicide charge and was on board with us immediately. The one thing that I wanted to find out from him was how he got involved with Malatesta in the first place. He said that he met Dante at one of the blackjack tables in the Venetian Hotel in Las Vegas. They struck up a conversation and Johnston mentioned his connection with a Mexican Bank. He told Dante that he could launder his money for a small fee of 5%. The rest was history.

My office wanted Johnstone to continue to work with Malatesta, while Joe and I got to Johns before Esposito did. He was told to continue to interest Dante and his associates in his innovate software program. He was directed to call me once a day to give me updates. It was impressed upon him that we needed to find Patrick Johns before Malatesta did.

As for Jack Shaw, he kept Joe and I hopping. Jack called Dante daily with updates on Johns' whereabouts. Shaw provided Dante subscriber information and an address. Once Dante received the information, he'd dispatch Peter Esposito to that address to deal with Johns.

Esposito who was now in Winston Salem, North Carolina. Esposito knocked on the front door of one of Johns' old girlfriend, who Johns had recently called. Joe and I actually saw Esposito walk up to the front door, ring the doorbell and speak to the woman. After a minute or so, he left the premises, got into his car and drove away. We immediately walked up to the front door and banged on it. She had a perplexed look when she opened the door and saw us standing there. We informed Miss Celia Brown of the gravity of the situation. We needed to find Patrick Johns before Esposito did. She admitted that Patrick stayed with her for a few days but left just hours before Esposito knocked on her door. Joe asked her, "Where he go?" She was forthright and said that she didn't know.

Johns had to know that Dante would eventually catch up with him and take his revenge. The bottom line is that he must have had a very good reason to take mob money and run. An exhausted search of Johns' background revealed that he had a son living in Montvale, NJ. If we found this out, I'm sure that Dante would find this out too. So, Joe and I decided to pay Johns' son a visit.

I'll never forget it, it was warm and sunny, when we drove up Johns' son's driveway and Joe parked his Ford Taurus. We slowly got out of the car and surveyed the ranch styled house, looking for anything out of the ordinary. We made our way up the driveway, to a set of brick stairs that led to the front door. Ringing the doorbell, a portly female, in her late forties, wearing a housecoat, answered the door. We identified ourselves and asked who she was. She told us that she was Kasey Johns. We told her that we were looking for her father-in-law, Patrick Johns. To our utter amazement, she said, "Patrick's in the basement. He's waiting for you. Follow me."
She took us through the living room and pointed to the cellar door off of the kitchen. With guns drawn, Joe and I slowly descended the cellar stairs into a lit basement as Kasey followed behind.

We scanned the basement and saw Patrick leaning against a pool table with his hands in the air. There was a 308 Remington riffle along with two pistols lying next to him on the pool table. What Patrick said put a shiver up my spine. "I had you in my sights as soon as you got out of your car. You're lucky that car looked like a police car, or I woulda' shot both of you."

It was just another day in the trenches. It was a blessing that I didn't take an undercover vehicle. If I had Johns might have thought it was Malatesta's men and shot Joe and I. After cuffing Johns and reading him his rights, I asked him, "Where's the eight hundred grand?" He pointed to a duffel bag under the pool table.

"You had to know that they'd be coming for you," Joe barked. "Why did you run with the money?" Joe went on to say, "We were one step ahead of Pete Esposito and that Malatesta had him marked for death."

"I know detective."

"Why'd you steal the mob's money?" I asked, "You had to know that they'd be coming for you."

"I'm dying! My heart is giving out." Johns blurted out. "I've got a bad heart and the doctor gave me six months to live. The money was for my son and his family. I needed to leave them something."

I shot a call into Captain Matthews and told him that Joe and I apprehended Patrick Johns and were bringing him in, along with the $800,000 that he stole from Malatesta. Of course, less several thousand dollars he spent on the run.

Walking him handcuffed into the prisoner's elevator felt like winning the lottery. Joe smirked as he pushed the elevator button to stop on the fourth floor. A few ADA's looked on as we escorted him down the hall to the interview room. ADA Falcone and Captain Matthews were waiting anxiously as we entered the room.

Falcone was very direct and laid everything out for Johns. His only option was to cooperate and testify truthfully, under oath about Dante Malatesta and Dante's money laundering operation. For his cooperation, Johns would be given a new identity and placed into the witness protection program.

Patrick agreed to sign a cooperation agreement with the District Attorney's office and was then debriefed for three days by ADA Falcone, Joe Nulligan and I. The information that Johns gave about Malatesta and his criminal activities were astounding. He laid out the all the crimes that Dante was involved in, the most startling revelation was that Dante reported directly to Carmine Corso. Wow! This opened up a flood gate of unanswered questions. Specifically, the unsolved murders of Gary Corso, Leonard Capolla and Gary's mistress, Claire Iverson.

ADA Falcone began, "Patrick, we insist you answer truthfully. If not, all bets are off and you'll be prosecuted for your part in the money laundering scheme. So, let me begin, who ordered the murders of Gary Corso and Leonard Capolla?"

Johns' reply shocked us all. The hairs on the back of my neck stood up. We stiffened up in our chairs and you could hear a pin drop in that room. Johns paused for a split second, took a deep breath and said, "Gary's father Carmine ordered his son's murder along with Leonard's. Claire Iverson was collateral damage. She happened to be in the wrong place at the wrong time when the hit went down."

Frozen in silence, trying to comprehend what was just said, we were stunned. The thought of a father having his own son murdered was unfathomable. "Why would Carmine kill his own son?" I blurted out.

"Because Gary and Lenny turned the business into a cash cow." Johns squawked. "Carmine is a greedy son of a bitch, one hundred percent evil and wanted the business back from Gary and Lenny. They refused to sell, so he had them killed. It's as simple as that."

"How do you know this?" Joe asked.

"I walked into a social club on 153rd Street in the Bronx and overheard him giving the contract to two black dudes who drove up from North Carolina."

Everyone, including Johns sat there in silence wondering how Carmine could have his son murdered.

"Of course, we'll have to verify all of this," ADA Falcone cried.

Nulligan snarled, "The fucking guy is diabolic, he has no soul."

The investigations ended with the arrest and convictions of all parties involved in the homicides and the laundering of the money from Malatesta's illegal business. Oh, and the mob wasn't ready to computerize their gambling operation. They couldn't wrap their heads around the computer age. Jack Shaw was convicted of commercial bribery of a telephone company employee and conspiracy to commit the murder. Peter Esposito was also convicted of conspiracy to commit murder. He's a three-time loser and is serving a life sentence. The phone company employee who provided Dante with Johns' cell phone information was fired. Carmine Corso, the monster, is serving a life sentence without the possibility of parole. As it turned out, Patrick Johns was a star witness for the state's cases. Shortly after several trials, he passed away from congestive heart failure.

As for the New Rochelle detective who put a gun to my head in Dana Corso's office, well I gotta settle up with him. This incident could have been disastrous and took my life. My mantra now is that life's a gift, so live it to the fullest.

Chapter Thirty-eight

I can't escape my childhood, even if I wanted to; it makes us who we are and I'm no exception. It's not easy for a guy like me to like and trust anyone but myself. I hate to keep repeating myself, but I guess the scars I received in grammar and high school, as a result of my learning disability, carried through into my personal and professional life. It's something I've learned to deal with on a daily basis. For example, when I was in uniform, before turning out on our assigned post, the squad sergeant would remind us to be mindful of illegally parked cars. I can't tell you how many license plate tags I screwed up because of my dyslexia. I'd write the plate number out of sequence and the letters backwards. So, when the vehicle received the parking fine, the owner of the car would go through the roof and complain to the police department. My department investigated and found that I was the patrol officer who wrote the ticket, reprimanded me and forbid me to write another parking ticket or moving violation.

It seems like everyone has their own personal agenda, whether they realize it or not. I remember how popular I became when people found out that I was cop. There were all the parties that Denise and I were invited to and the well-wishers that wanted to stay on my good side. Inevitably there would be one of the party goers who had the speeding ticket they wanted squashed, or the disgruntled guy who was having a problem with his neighbor who constantly blocked his driveway and wanted me to do something about it. Of course, I'd give the person lip service, but that was it.

Sometimes my intervention was warranted. Most memorable was the son of a friend who was being harassed by his next-door neighbor. The kid was tattooed and drove a motorcycle. Like the old saying goes, you can't judge a book by its cover. The young man, in his mid-twenties, was hard working and a very nice person. He'd go out of his way for anyone. The kids neighbor, a retired laborer, was observed on a few occasions by another neighbor flattening tires on the young man's motorcycle. I surmise that the aging neighbor didn't like the young man's looks and tattoos on both arms. As I said, Johnny, was hard working and worked as a lineman for the local phone company. On many a morning, me, Johnny and his father John would have breakfast in John's kitchen. John asked his son if anything was bothering him. His father finally forced it out of him. Eventually out of frustration, he confided that his neighbor had been harassing him for some time. John Sr. asked me if there was anything I could do to rectify the problem. "Yeah," I said. "I'll have a heart to heart with the low-life."

It wasn't long before I paid the asshole a visit. One morning, I knocked on the neighbor's door and we had a face-to-face discussion, I nearly slapped him in the mouth with my shield. I told him, straight out, that if the kid next door had another flat tire or was to have any other property damage, he'd have hell to pay with me and the cops on patrol in his neighborhood. Make no mistake about it; I get a huge charge out of putting a creep like this guy, in his place. The very next day, the scumbag brought over a tray of baked Ziti to Johnny and said that if there was anything, he could do for him, to just please let him know.

It seems that I have a knack for dealing with assholes. As a kid growing up, I was always on the street and as the phrase goes, became street-smart. I knew who was harmless and who I had to keep an eye on. The streets of New York are their own learning experience. If you can survive on the streets, you can survive anywhere. Again, this carried over into my professional life. I knew who was dangerous and who wasn't.

Even in the mob, I was taught to protect myself, specifically from the cops. Mob guys hated cops and informers. The first thing they taught me was to think cop as soon as I opened my eyes in the morning. I talked about Freddy Spina earlier in the book. He was my sponsor into the mob. What he told me made a lot of sense. "Frankie, the cops have their job to do and we have ours." Freddy taught me how to pick up a tail, which has stayed with me. Freddy said, "if the cops get a line on you, they'll try to follow you to see where you're going and who you're meeting. That's how they build a case against you. Your side view mirrors are your best friend. Use them as soon as you pull into traffic. You'll be able to see the cars that pull out behind you. If a car pulls out behind you, keep an eye on it. Drive around the block a few times to see if he's still behind you. If he is, it's a sure bet that you're being followed. Don't take him anywhere that concerns our business,"

After the arrests were made, it was no secret that Freddy was the one who brought a cop into Calise's street crew. They had to set an example of him. Freddy was beaten within an inch of his life and he nearly died. It haunts me, even until today. He was nearly killed because of me.

The only consolation I have is that Freddy chose that life and knew exactly what he was getting himself into. I think that what we stand for makes a big difference on how we do as a society and a country as a whole. It makes us who we are as a nation.

Chapter Thirty-nine

Ya never know when somebody is gonna go bad. I've already mentioned that you can never trust an informant. When their backs are to the wall, they'll try to throw you under the bus. Deputy Chief Achim took me aside one day and said, "Be careful Frankie, I know that informants are a necessary evil, but sooner or later they'll try to jam you up."

One informant that sticks in my mind is a convicted narcotics felon that I worked with from time to time. His name was Ranaldo Cambrari, he's short, bald and looks like a bowling ball. Ranaldo was a mover and shaker in the drug world. He had connections to all major drug dealers that hung out in the NYC night clubs. We'd occasionally meet in the coffee shop down the street from his building to discuss potential targets. The guy lives a one-bedroom apartment with his girlfriend, in the Woodlawn section of the Bronx. I got a good look at his girlfriend a few months ago. She's also short, fat with dark eyes and jet-black hair. She's a real Colombian brute. Camila, in her early twenties, answered the door. She was dressed in a flimsy nightgown that rendered the rolls of her belly fat. I had to look away.

One morning, Ranaldo called me and asked to meet him at his house instead of the coffee shop. He said that he met a coke dealer he wants me to meet.

Camila again answered the door. Her dark black eyes seemed to study every inch of me. "He's in the bedroom Frank. Go right in."

The apartment was unkempt. I stepped over clothes and cases of bottled water and made my way down the short hallway to the bedroom. I knocked a few times, but Ranaldo didn't answer, so I opened it. It was 10:15 a.m. and he was still in bed. When he saw me standing over him, he yawned and said, "Good morning."

"Ranaldo, why are you still in bed? Aren't you feeling well?"

He looked at me and smiled. "Look in my closet, the top shelf. I've got something for you."

The closet door was open. I looked in and gazed up to the top shelf. Wow! I'll never forget what I saw staring me in the face. There was a stack of money, tightly bound, about twenty inches high and tied with butcher twine.

"Take it down Frank. It's for you."

I grabbed the stack of money and placed it down on the bed. I fingered through the mound of twenty dollars bills. "What'd ya mean it's for me?" I stammered.

"Frankie, there's $50,000 dollars there. I want you to have it."

"Where the fuck? Where'd you get it?"

"My mother sold one of her apartment buildings in the city and it's part of my inheritance. The money's yours."

"Mine?"

Everything came flooding back to me. My family values. What my father said to me about being honest and protecting my family's good name. I was just scrapping by on a cop's salary and I'll admit it, his offer was tempting. When all is said and done, I knew what the financial deal was when I signed on to become a cop. I wasn't gonna get rich. The money wasn't mine and I'd be damned to take it. I've never taken a penny in my life that didn't belong to me. I hate to say it, but the Feds are always looking to bust a dirty cop.

What I said next must have shocked Ranaldo. "What you just did, motherfucker, crossed the line. I don't give a flying fuck about you or your money. I'll bet you dollars to donuts that the FBI is listening in on our conversation right now. You've got yourself in a jam and you're trying to dig yourself out of the mess you're in by telling them that I take money. Ranaldo, if I walked out with the fifty large, I'd be cuffed an arrested by the Feds as soon as I hit the sidewalk. Fuck you, we're done."

Chapter Forty

The situation with Ranaldo Cambrari comes with the territory as stressful as it was. One of my C.I.'s was a guy by the name of Angelo Vitulli. Angelo peddled cocaine for a living, but he sold it to the wrong guy, me. He worked for me as my C.I. (Confidential Informant) for a while, until he satisfied his beef and avoided prison.

Vitulli was a victim of the drug trade, selling the shit to support his heroin habit. Unfortunately, Angelo just put himself back in the slam for selling cocaine to another undercover cop. Since he has worked with me and trusts me, he called me, looking to get him out from under from his latest mess. The problem is that Vitulli is now a predicate felon, which means he's already been convicted of a felony and the statue states that the court has no choice but to sentence him to state prison.

I happen to be in the office late one afternoon when my desk phone rang. The operator asked if I'd accept a call from Angelo Vitulli, an inmate at the Westchester County Jail. Of course I'd accept the call.

"Hey Pete, looks like you fucked up again. What's up?"

"Yeah Frank, I got myself into trouble again. I sold a 1/8th of a Kilo of coke to a narc who works for the Westchester County PD. I need your help."

"Ya know, there's not much I can do. I hope that you realize that you're a predicate felon. It's gonna depend on what you can give me and that might not be enough for the judge to give you a pass."

"I know, I know, Frank, but whatever you can do will help. What I have just might do the trick."

Guys like Angelo always kept me in action. It's what makes me tick. "So what,d ya have?"

"I've been keeping this under my hat, for just a situation like this. More than a dozen years ago, I knew a guy, Paul Piccolo abducted his two-year-old son from his estranged wife Connie. The kid was still drinking from a bottle when his father took him. They're now living in an apartment in the Bronx. Paul has been moving around from state to state to stay under the police's radar. He's been home schooling his son Sam and giving piano lessons to make ends meet."

"How did you find out that Piccolo is back in town?"

"Frank, I have eyes and ears on the street too."

"Angelo, give me some time to check this out. Call me tomorrow at about the same time. I'll see if your information is on the money."

As soon as I hung up, I began to check out Vitulli's story. Right off the bat, I hit a home run. The National Center for Missing and Exploited Children found Samuel Piccolo on their list of missing children. I also established that there was an outstanding federal warrant charging his father with unlawful flight to avoid prosecution. He also faces a charge of first-degree custodial interference in the State of Connecticut. When the kid was abducted, he was living in Stanford with his mother. The case stems from a 2001, court approved visit between his then two-year old son, whose mother had legal custody. Piccolo never returned the boy, who at one point was thought to be living in Colorado, according to an FBI affidavit.

The next day, right on time, Angelo called. I told him that his information was on target. What I needed to know was where Piccolo was living.

"Frank, I got Paul's address, but I gotta know that I'll get credit when you pick the guy up."

"Look Angelo, you know me. You know that I ain't gonna stiff you. Whatever I can do to help your situation, I'll do. Remember though, no promises."

"Okay. But you gotta know that the kids' father barely lets his son out of the apartment. The guy's paranoid. He sees cops in his sleep."

Angelo seemed to be hedging. "C'mon Angelo, what's the address? You're wasting my time."

"Their living in a 4th floor apartment at 9556 East 183rd Street, in the Bronx. Again, I need assurances that I'm gonna get credit for the arrest."

"Relax Angelo. I said I'll do my best for you with the judge. Sit tight, I'll get back to you."

The very next day, at 6:00 a.m., armed with an old FBI photograph of Paul Piccolo, Joe Nulligan and I set up a surveillance on the East 183rd Street apartment building. Our eyes were glued on the building for two days. On the third day, at about 12:30 p.m., a sliding glass door opened from an apartment on the fourth floor. A male stepped out from the apartment onto the balcony. Looking at Piccolo's photo, there was no doubt that the guy who stepped onto the balcony was Paul Piccolo. Piccolo, now in his late forties, looked gaunt. His long dark hair grazed his shoulders as he walked. Not long after, another male walked out. He was in his late teens with short chopped dark hair, thin framed, about 5 feet-ten inches tall. They were talking as Paul lit a cigarette and gazed out onto East 183rd Street. We needed to get the correct apartment number to seal the deal. After about ten minutes of chatting, they both walked back into the apartment. Paul looked as if he locked the sliding the door once inside.

Joe and I tossed things around for a while, deciding the best way to get into the apartment number. We concluded that I'd enter the building, take the elevator to the 4th floor and put my ear to each door and attempt to locate which apartment Paul and his son were in. We had a pretty good idea which two or so it was from counting the balconies.

I walked the short distance to the front entrance of the building, into the austere lobby and took the elevator to the fourth floor. As soon as the elevator door opened, a few doors down from the elevator, Paul Piccolo was leaving his apartment, apartment 4J. I had a surge of energy thinking that Piccolo would soon be in handcuffs. He didn't pay me any attention as we passed each other in the hallway and he got into the elevator. I gave him a few minutes before I left the building and hooked up with Nulligan. I slid into the passenger side of Joe's Ford Taurus, excited and ready for action. "Joe, we got him! Apartment 4J. Did you see him walk out of the building?"

"No Frankie, sorry I didn't see him."

Joe pulled the car closer to the building, parking just a stone's throw away from the main entrance. Just as he turned the ignition off, Piccolo walked past us, carrying what looked like a bag of groceries and entered the building. Bingo, he's ours.

Joe popped the trunk and we suited up with vests and blue raid jackets that had the word police inscribed in large yellow letters on the front and back. Joe then grabbed a fifty-pound battering ram and we made our way into the building. We passed a few tenants leaving the building. We didn't have to wait long for the elevator. Joe and I stood in front of apartment 4J for a few seconds, then gave each other a thumbs up as Joe swung the ram three or four times into the door, knocking it off its hinges. The door flew open into the living room. We found Paul and his son Sam cowering behind a couch. We yelled, "Hands up, get down on your knees with your hands cupped behind your heads!"

With guns drawn, the Piccolo's complied without incident. After handcuffing both of them and pulling them up off of the floor, Paul grumbled, "What the hell is this all about?"

I calmly replied, "You're under arrest on a federal warrant for kidnapping your son Sam some fifteen years ago. And you're also charged with custodial interference in Connecticut."

With that, Sam looked over at his father, dropped his head and shook his head no. Joe and I escorted the Piccolo's out of the building to Joe's car and placed them in the back seat. I radioed ahead to our office, letting them know that we were coming in with one prisoner and a kidnap victim.
The next day, Paul was turned over to the FBI. He was arraigned in federal court on the kidnapping charge and was awaiting arraignment on the state charge in Connecticut. During his federal arraignment, it was learned that Sam had never been enrolled in school or inoculated against childhood diseases. Sam's father was remanded into federal custody without bail. The missing boy was thin but as I said, apparently healthy. He was reunited with his mother after the arraignment.

Paul Piccolo plead guilty to federal and state charges and was sentenced to three years in federal prison. After his sentence was severed, Paul was turned over to the State of Connecticut and served another year behind bars. As for Angelo Vitulli, I was able to get him off the hook. But, as fate would have it, six months later, he died from a heroin overdose.

Chapter Forty-one

All work and no play makes Jack a dull boy or so they say. I guess I'm like most men, enjoying the company of an attractive woman is one of the true joys in life. Denise Mackenzie and I having been living together now for a while and our connection was at a fever pitch. My days were occupied with the dregs of society, but most nights were filled with intimacy.

The night after the Piccolo matter was settled, I got home a little after seven. Denise wasn't home yet and the apartment was hauntingly quiet. I pulled off my sweatshirt, threw it on the couch and turned on the radio. There was an open bottle of Pino Grigio on the coffee table. It wasn't stale yet, so I poured a glass and plopped down on the couch to relax. Finally, I could have a few minutes of peace and calm and not think about my job. I began to think about why I can't sit still and leave anything undone. I guess it stems from my disability (dyslexia). The inability to make everything and everyone around me perfect; like I'm not. I know I gotta be hard to live with, but Denise seems to get me and understands my idiosyncrasies.

It was after 8:00 p.m. when Denise walked in with a bottle of Chardonnay tucked under her arm. She wasted no time uncorking it. "I bought a bottle of wine and some cheese to pick on." I guess you're hungry?' I heard the cork pop from the kitchen. She strutted back into the living room with the wine, cheese and two crystal glasses sitting on a small ornate silver serving tray. She carefully placed it on the coffee table, snuggled down beside me, threw her arms around my neck and kissed me.

"Hey," I said, somewhat surprised, "Is there a special occasion or something?"

Her eyes said it all. She pressed herself against me and softly began to massage my inner thigh. With a sultry look she said gently, "Honey, every day is a special occasion with you." and grabbed the bottle of chardonnay, filling the two glasses. Our eyes were centered on one another. We raised our glasses and made a lover's toast as we clinked our glasses. I was completely aroused; sparks were flying between us. I knew we were heading to the bedroom. She put her glass down, again, she drew herself closer into me. Our bodies touching, her lips inches away from mine and then kissed me gently. I grabbed her tiny waist. Her body couldn't get any closer. I felt her body go limp. She shifted her head back, just enough so that I could feel her breath on my face. She sighed, "We'll get through everything together. Frankie, I love you."

I then gently pushed her down onto the couch as she surrendered herself to me. I kissed her lips as though I could devour her. Articles of our clothing flew all over the room as I tore them off. I passionately undressed her piece by piece. Her body was on fire. As the song lyrics say, Your Body is a Wonderland. Soft moans escaped her mouth as I explored every tantalizing inch of her. Our sexual chemistry was like no other. She whispered again, "Oh Frankie, I love you so much. I want us to be together always." I wished that our love making could go on forever. I didn't want the titillating pleasure to end, but our overpowering sexual feeling mounted to such a degree that we were unable to control our passion any longer, exploding in ecstasy. As we lay there, exhausted, there was no doubt in my mind that I wanted to share the rest of my life with her. "Denise," I whispered, "I'm completely in love with you. I've never had this with anyone else." She took hold of my face, kissing me softly and saying, "Yes, yes Frankie, I know." Our chemistry was so great that there isn't anything that could keep us apart. It must have been written in the stars that we were meant to be together. I was going to ask her to marry me, but I was afraid that she might say no.

Chapter Forty-two

Most of the cops I know are hit hard emotionally when one of us is killed in the line of duty. Every time I attended an Inspector's funeral, that's what we called them, I'm thinking, I can't wait to fuckin' retire so I don't have to attend another cop's funeral. I remember the last one I attended. It was a bright and sunny spring morning when about 1,000 of us were gathered outside Holy Name Catholic Church in White Plains, NY. The lieutenant in charge of the NYPD Honor Guard called everyone to attention, as the flag draped coffin was carried out by the pallbearers, all who worked with Michael Gurney, in 2 squad of the Eastchester Police Department. His coffin was followed by Michael's wife, his two small kids, family and close friends. We saluted Michael, then came to attention as his coffin was placed into the hearse.

Michael was eulogized by the clergy, politicians, the chief of police and his brother. They all said that he was a dedicated family man and public servant. His name will be engraved on the police memorial that stands in front of the courthouse. But when push comes to shove, Michael was dead and his wife and kids had to go home without him. They say that time heals all, but for Michael's wife and children it would be a long hard road ahead for them. I just wonder if the public really know the sacrifices that our families and friends make.

Funerals like Michael's never leave my mind. It's heart-wrenching just thinking about them. I'll do everything I can not to be carried out of a church in a coffin like Mike was. After Michael's burial, I started to carry a 12-gauge sawed off shot gun, loaded with double 0 buckshot and kept under the front seat of my car. It was definitely the great equalizer. This might sound odd, but me and Nulligan had a saying when it came to locking up bad guys who wanted to go the hard way. "Stop, "Bang," halt, police!"

Chapter Forty-three

After the shooting death of police officer Michael Gurney, I realized that I was missing out on so much of life, especially by not having the courage to marry Denise MacKenzie. We were meant for each other and it didn't make any sense to waste any more time, I needed to make our relationship official. As the saying goes, behind every successful man is a great woman. Denise fit that bill and so much more.

Because of being financially strapped as a result of child support and alimony payments I wasn't able to afford to buy Denise an engagement ring. My mom recommended Hakins' Jewelers on Main Street in Portchester, NY. She said that she'd dealt with them in the past and that they were honorable people to deal with. So, one Saturday afternoon, I paid them a visit to pick out a wedding band. It was the best I could do at the time, but as soon as my fiscal situation changed, I planned to buy Denise a diamond engagement ring.

Hakins' was owned and operated by a Jewish family who've been dealing in jewelry and precious stones for over 75 years. The owner, Abe, a low-pressure salesman, 6' feet, slender, in his mid-forties and dressed in light colored dress slacks, white button-down shirt, opened at the collar and gold rimmed glasses that sat on the edge of his nose. I introduced myself when I walked in and said that my mother Inez recommended his store. He was very cordial and asked what I was looking for. I told him that I was proposing to my girlfriend and looking to purchase a wedding band. "I'll show you a variety of rings."as he slid open a section of the glass counter and took out a brown velveteen tray and place it down on the counter. After looking at several rings, I settled on a 1 ½ carat diamond wedding band in 14k white gold. It retails for $3,500, but Abe said because he remembered that my father's family came from Portchester, I could have the ring for $2,800, a 20% discount.

I was extremely nervous about getting married again, but excited at the same time. Committing to one person for the rest of your life is a big deal for me, especially since my first marriage failed miserably. I'm a romantic at heart and wanted to propose in a romantic place in New York City.

I asked around and a friend, who works in the corporate world, mentioned Bryant Park on 6th Avenue and 42nd Street. She's been there many times and mentioned how beautiful it was, especially in spring and summer, with the vast variety of trees and flowers. I gave it a look-see and the place was idyllic. People came to relax on blankets or benches, sharing a bottle of wine and pickings of grapes and cheese. It was paved with bike paths and were lined with the most beautiful flowers. It was the perfect setting and I knew that Denise would love it.

It was a warm and sunny Sunday afternoon in June, when we arrived at the park. We were like two kids as we walked in, looking at the fresh flowers and the sycamore tress blowing in the warm breeze. We passed a few lovers cuddling on blankets near a gazebo in the middle of the park and found a quiet place on at the east end of the park. I asked Denise, "Do you like it?" as we laid the blanket down on the grass. "I love it!" she replied. She was taking in the view of the 42nd St. Park, the landscape, the skyline, she was captivated. It was a far cry from the dirt filled venues I was used to.

Denise opened my wicker basket, it was brimming with Dom Perignon Champagne, assorted grapes, Fontinella cheese, sesame crackers and two chocolate truffles. Denise was a bit taken aback by the expensive champagne and said, "Really Frankie, Dom Perignon?" She had no idea that I was about to propose to her. There was ice in a freezer bag and two champagne glasses that I'd placed in the basket. Immediately, I popped the cork and poured the bubbly as we toasted each other, clicking our glasses before leaning in for a kiss.

"Frankie, this is so romantic. I really do love it, thank you for bringing me here."

As we picked on the grapes and cheese, I stood, reached into my pocket, took out the small red velveteen box, then got down on one knee and opened the box to the stunning diamond wedding band. I took a deep breath, looking into Denise's eyes, not knowing her reply and asked her to marry me.

"Denise, you're the love of my life and my soul mate. I can't imagine living another day without you as my wife. Say we'll spend the rest of our lives together; will you marry me?"

She jumped up, threw herself on me and roared, "Frankie, of course I'll marry you!" I was stunned and thrilled! "Yes, yes, yes, I'll marry you!" Tears streamed down her face as the outcry of congratulations and applause came from the surrounding blankets. Now the only thing left to do, or so I thought, was to set our wedding date. From a woman's perspective, there's so much more to a wedding than I could ever have imagined. There's the invitations, guest lists, the venue, the flowers and of course Denise's wedding dress. This was all new to me. I was on the road to a new life with the woman I loved and a promise of a bright future.

Chapter Forty-four

The evening before our wedding the entire bridal party attended the wedding rehearsal at Corpus Christi church in Port Chester, New York. Most of my aunts, uncles and cousins have been married there. The church was built in 1945 by my father and his three brothers. They did much of the exterior stonework and the interior plastering of the building. They were taught their trade from my grandfather Carmine, a master European craftsman, who had died before I was born. So, you can see why I wanted to tie the knot there. The church has so much sentimental history for me and my family.

Fittingly, because of the emotional attachment I had to the church, Denise loved the idea of marrying there. Loving Denise the way I did, when it came right down to it, marrying again scared the living hell out of me. Setting my fears aside for a moment, Denise has stood by me through thick and thin, through all the trials and tribulations of living with an undercover cop. So far on our journey together, she's experienced, firsthand, some of the bumps and bruises, the stress and anxiety along the seedy and dangerous world I worked in, I loved her courage she mustered to share in our unique relationship that took her into my sometimes dark and perilous existence. She was going to be in for the ride of her life.

My brother Rich was my best man and Ace Lifrieri, Angel and Joe Nulligan were my groomsmen. These were the guys I counted on for loyalty, friendship and support. Through thick and thin they never let me down. They're men who have been tested by flames and never flinched in the fire. Denise had asked Nulligan's girlfriend, Jessica Carbone to be her maid of honor and her Aunt Margret to give her away.

I remember the day like it was yesterday. The limo was late to pick up me and the guys at my apartment in Bronxville. It was a thirty-minute ride to the church for the 2:00 pm service and it was already 1:15 p.m. Denise, her bridesmaids Catie, Francesca, Jessica, Jessica's nice, Jennifer and Jessica's nephew Ryan were our ring bearers. They had spent the night at Jessica's apartment in New Rochelle and were already at the church.

On the ride over to the church, my mind began to play tricks on me. As crazy as it sounds, I began to wonder if this was the right thing for me to do it again. Denise and my relationship was as good as it gets and I didn't want to ruin it by getting married.

We arrived at the church at exactly 1:45 p.m. Father Nino Cavallo was waiting impatiently at the side entrance of a packed church. He rushed me and the groomsmen into the sacristy. "It will be a minute Frank." Father Nino said with a smile. He then asked my brother to stay, then asked Joe, Ace and Angel to step out into the church by the alter. I spotted a red velvet kneeler over in the corner of the room. I thought that it would be a good idea to say a few prayers before this life altering event. I must have gone into a trance like state because I didn't hear Father Nino say, "Frank, it's time to go." He must have said it three or four times. When I finally heard him and tried to get up, my legs wouldn't move. I couldn't stand up. It must have been psychosomatic or something. "Richie, I need your help! Father Nino yelped. "Grab an arm!" They literally dragged me up from the kneeler and out to the alter in front of the waiting congregation. I stood at the alter and looked towards the front of the church. The organist began to play as Catie, Francesca, Jennifer and Ryan stood waiting for the procession to begin. The doors to the church opened and Angel and Joe unrolled the white runner down the center aisle.

Denise stood there in her Monique Lhuillier designer wedding dress. A silk mermaid style grown with a sweetheart neckline and a gorgeous floor length veil. She was the most beautiful woman I ever saw. Suddenly, all my fears of marriage vanished. What was I thinking? I couldn't imagine I had any doubts about marrying her. She is the most beautiful person inside and out that I've ever met.

Catie and Francesca began to sprinkle red rose petals on the white runner as Spencer and Jennifer carried our wedding rings. Denise's Aunt Margret, a beautiful woman in her own right, began to walk my bride to be down the aisle to my waiting arms. As I watched Denise gracefully glide down the aisle, I knew that we would maintain the spark of love until death do us part. Denise's Aunt Margret, now in her early sixties, elegantly dressed in a yellow taffeta, floor length gown, lifted Denise's veil and handed me her hand. She was so beautiful, the thought of spending the rest of my life with her was overwhelming. I'll never forget that feeling of love. We tenderly exchanged vows with the promise to love and respect one another as Father Nino pronounced us man and wife. "Frank, you may now kiss your bride." to a raucous round of applause and wolf whistles. We left the church with kisses and handshakes. Our limo's took us to a Country Club in Pleasantville, NY for cocktails, hors d' oeuvres and dinner.

We decided to honeymoon in Italy, spending some time in my grandfather Guarino's town of Rimini, in northern Italy.

I have no regrets choosing a career in law enforcement. I've had the rare opportunity to meet the best and the worst people that society has to offer. The only regrets I have are purely personal ones.

The End!

About the author

 Frank retired as Chief of Detectives from the Westchester County District Attorney's Office, NY. Before rising through the ranks, he spent most of his career working deep undercover assignments involving organized crime investigations. He has been featured in the law enforcement segment of The Real Sopranos documentary by Class Films, London, England, TNT's Family Values the Mob & the Movies and interviewed by Juan Williams on NPR's Talk of the Nation regarding Mob Images in Popular Culture. Mr. Santorsola is available for speaking engagements. Please contact Miranda Books Inc. at: frank@franksantrorsla.com.

Made in the USA
Columbia, SC
26 August 2021

44401291R00100